i so
don't do
spooky

i so don't do spooky

Barrie Summy

SCHOLASTIC INC.

New York Toronto London Auckland
Sydney Mexico City New Delhi Hong Kong

No part of this publication may be reproduced, stored in a retrieval system, or transmitted in any form or by any means, electronic, mechanical, photocopying, recording, or otherwise, without written permission of the publisher. For information regarding permission, write to Random House Children's Books, a division of Random House, Inc., 1745 Broadway, New York, NY 10019.

ISBN 978-0-545-28839-2

12 11 10 9 8 7 6 5 4 3 2 1   11 12 13 14 15 16/0

Printed in the U.S.A.   40

First Scholastic printing, January 2011

For Norma and Tommy,
the best in-laws a girl
could wish for

acknowledgments

Rachel Vater is a very, very amazing individual. From hand holding to brainstorming to agent wheeling and dealing, she does it all. I only wish we lived closer to each other, so we could hang out.

I'm not exactly sure how I ended up with the most talented, most brilliant, most creative editor in the whole wide world. Wendy Loggia, you are incredible. Seriously, I can't gush enough.

Thank you also to the entire genius team at Delacorte Press, including Beverly Horowitz, my publisher; Marci Senders, designer extraordinaire; Heather Lockwood Hughes, eagle-eyed copy editor; and Krista Vitola, Wendy's right-hand person.

I'm forever indebted to my dedicated and gifted critique group, Denny's Chicks: Kelly Hayes, Kathy Krevat and Sandy Levin. Where would I be without you guys? Oh yeah, drinking coffee and eating veggie omelets all by myself.

Heartfelt and humongous thanks to Owen, Katie, Jocelyn, Hannah, Alexander and Melanie for providing such interesting material(!), but mostly for just being beaucoup de fun! Always be loving and kind to your mothers. They are the best sisters around.

i so don't do spooky

chapter
one

I have an überwonderful life!

Überwonderful spelled J-o-s-h M-o-r-t-o-n.

Josh Morton. Cute, cool, amazing eighth grader at Saguaro Middle School, Phoenix, Arizona. The same Josh Morton who just happens to be my boyfriend. Has been since spring break. Which today totals exactly two months of heart happiness.

On this rocking Friday morning in May, Josh and I are gonna hang together at the lunch tables before first bell. His idea. He wants to tell me something. He forgot our one-month anniversary, so I bet he's got plans extraordinaire for this one.

I slide a few pink hangers across the bar in my closet, stopping at my watermelon-colored skirt with swirly black designs. Watermelon skirt + black Lycra T-shirt + black leggings + peachish ballet slippers = adorable fashion statement.

My makeup is done—that is, the minuscule amount I'm allowed to wear—but I still have my hair to tackle. And I will absolutely, one hundred percent be on time and perfectly put together for my romantic rendezvous.

"Sherry!"

The Ruler's calling me. My fairly new and obnoxious stepmother. Like I even need a stepmother. As it is, I can barely handle my own mom. Not to mention that The Ruler teaches at *my* middle school. Mega embarrassing. *And* she's my first-period computer teacher. Mega mega embarrassing.

"Sherry!"

"I'm getting ready."

"Sherry!"

Ack. She's right outside my room. I swing open the door. Staring into the hall, I widen my eyes with attitude. "Yeah?"

Tall, thin and decked out in shades of golden brown, The Ruler's a walking, talking french fry. She glances at my eyes and pauses. After a deep yoga-ish breath, she says, "I've lost my school keys again." Her hands flutter in the air. "You have to help me find them."

What is the deal? Lately, the woman's been losing

everything. Which is way weird given her personality. I mean, the entire school doesn't call her The Ruler for nothing. Besides the fact that she stands inhumanly straight like she's got a ruler up her back, she's also Queen of the Control Freaks. In her class, your binder better have all the notes and homework dated and in chrono order. Or she'll shave points off your grade.

Living with The Ruler is no Laffy Taffy. It's like when you try on those strung-together shoes at Target. You can't take big steps; you definitely can't run; you can't really tell how you feel about the footwear. Well, with the gazillion rules in our house, I only get to take teeny-tiny steps that don't include TV on weekdays, MySpace anytime or unlimited texting. I won't even start ragging on the health food I'm forced to eat.

In short, living with The Ruler makes me want to bust out a pair of scissors and cut that shoe string.

"Sherry," The Ruler says, "let's start looking for my keys downstairs."

Hinting hugely, I wave my clothes in the air and nod toward the door. "I gotta leave in twelve and a half minutes, and I'm still in my pj's."

"Twelve and a half minutes?" She frowns, her forehead turning into a crinkle-cut fry. "Classes don't start for over an hour. Anyway, I can give you a ride."

I am officially stating here and now that I will never be caught entering or exiting the passenger side of her forest green hybrid on Saguaro property. Nuh-uh. Not happening.

"Sherry, hurry up," she bosses. "I barely got any sleep last night with those phone calls again."

That's the second time we've gotten phone calls in the middle of the night where the person doesn't say anything. Probably a student she's failing. "What about Sam?" I say. "He's better at finding stuff than me anyway." Very brilliant suggestion on my part, as I need my eight-year-old brother to vacate our shared bathroom so I can do something, anything with my wild porcupine hair.

"You take the living room," The Ruler says.

I glance at my clock radio and quickly calculate key-hunting time + dressing time + hair time + sprinting-to-school time. I huff, "Fine, but we better be fast." Pounding on the bathroom door, I shriek, "Sam!"

The three of us motor downstairs. I'm leading the pack, boogying on fast-forward like I'm Halloween-candy hyper. We separate to search different rooms. The sec I hit the living room, I'm whirling, I'm twirling, eyes darting. I flip couch cushions, toss newspapers and magazines, kick up throw rugs.

Nada. It's like the keys grew wings and fluttered off.

All high-pitched, The Ruler calls from the kitchen, "Did you find anything?"

"Nothing in the office!" Sam yells.

"Ditto for the living room," I say.

Sam wheelies from the hall over to me, bashing his shins on the coffee table. Eyes round like yo-yos, he scans the room.

The Ruler hurries in. Her jaw drops. "Sherry, did you have to destroy the place?"

"Just trying to be thorough," I snap. Thorough and fast. So I can get back to my real life.

She closes her eyes and does the slow deep-breathing thing again.

Maybe she's enrolled in a yoga class I don't know about.

"Okay." She opens her eyes. "Now for the upstairs. Sam, you take the bathroom. Sherry and I'll handle my bedroom."

"No," I wail. "I just want to go to school."

Both The Ruler and Sam stare at me like I've gone crazy. Because that statement? It's so not me.

"Paula"—Sam runs his fingers through his half-gelled hair—"where'd you find your keys on Friday?"

"In the microwave."

"In the microwave," he repeats thoughtfully. "And the other day, they were in the fridge?"

The Ruler nods.

He grabs her hand. "Let's check the kitchen."

Like a rocket, I zoom upstairs to my bedroom. I throw off my pj's, pull on my clothes, then jam my feet into the ballet slippers. Despite my desperate

5

hurry, I manage to mutter sweet nothings to my beloved bala sharks, who are zipping around the aquarium, dodging fake plants and castles.

"What do you think Josh is getting me for our anniversary?" I ask the fish.

Zip. Zip. Zip.

"I agree. It'll be something perfect and Josh-like."

Zip. Zip. Zip.

Finally, I clip back my hair because, well, I'm out of time. With a wide swinging arc, my backpack is up off the bedroom floor and—

Yikeserama.

It isn't closed.

Books thud to the floor, papers flutter, gel pens roll. On my stomach, I grab as much junk as I can and shove it back in.

Then I'm bounding down the stairs, two and three at a time, backpack slapping at my spine like a giant flyswatter. My fingers are crossed that I don't trip and break a leg or an arm or a tooth. Given the way my morning has panned out so far, this stair-hopping is literally living life on the edge.

Hands on hips, and her face cranked up in a badcop expression, The Ruler guards the front door.

I skid to a halt only inches from her.

Out of the corner of my eye, I spot Sam at the archway to the kitchen. I try to catch his attention, but he's avoiding my gaze, staring down at his big toe poking through his holey sock. Something is very wrong.

From her skirt pocket, The Ruler pulls a round brass key ring.

"Great. You found them," I say.

She crosses her bony arms, the key ring jingling next to a pointy elbow. "They were in the pantry by the soda."

My stomach begins a slow downward spiral.

"You know *I* don't drink soda, and I've weaned your *father* off the poison. I buy your *brother* organic juice boxes." The Ruler joggles the keys so that they clink together like wind chimes.

My stomach hits the tile floor.

It's so totally obvious what's going on.

chapter
two

Unfortunately for me, I deal with two not-completely-normal mothers.

First, there's The Ruler, my stepmother, who's all of a sudden losing it. Even more disturbing, she's blaming her crazy behavior on me.

The Ruler's usual rational, orderly self left the building a while ago. Ever since the school robotics club started back up this year with her as teacher-mentor. Now she's frazzled and disorganized and, apparently, nutzoid. Like thinking I would purposely hide her keys. Hello! I am so not a practical joker.

Second, there's my real mother. A cop with the Phoenix police department, Mom was killed over a year and a half ago during a drug bust. She enrolled in the Academy of Spirits so she could watch over Sam and me. And learn to watch over the rest of the world, which is what the Academy trains ghosts for.

The thing is, while she was a dynamo cop, Mom has, well, struggled with the ghost thing. Just a couple of months ago, I had to help her solve a mystery to raise her in-the-toilet grades and save her from being expelled. I can always hear her and smell the coffee scent that trails after her. I can sometimes feel her.

But I never see her. Which is bugging me more and more.

I sigh. "Paula, I just wanna get to school early to see Josh. It's our anniversary."

The Ruler smiles and her plainish face lights up.

In her own Rulerish way, she's got a sentimental heart thumping away in her chest. She definitely dotes on my dad, always baking him heavy bran stuff, like carrot muffins. She's been kinda down and sluggish with him gone to Las Vegas for a couple of weeks of sales meetings. Morphing into instant single mom can't be easy. From the gazillion phone calls, I know my dad's missing her and us.

"Your two-month anniversary?" The Ruler's eyes twinkle.

I tilt my head and close an eye. Peach blush, five or six coats of navy mascara and bright lipstick would totally spiff up her look. "Yeah."

"Fine. But, Sherry, please leave my keys alone."

I start to protest how it's her, not me, then snap my mouth shut. I just want outta here. Pronto. "Deal."

I push open the front door. With a long Olympic stride, I'm quickly halfway across the porch. Then, I trip.

Over a bouquet of bright-colored flowers.

Josh must've arranged for an early-morning delivery to surprise me. How incredibly sweet. How incredibly romantic. How incredibly grown-up. I grab the bouquet, poke my nose down in the flowers and take a big, huge sniff of love. Ahhh. Josh is so the best. Then I pluck out the oh-so-cute mini envelope, shove it in my pocket and lovingly lay the flowers back on the porch. I can't tote them around with me all day and I certainly don't have time to do the whole vase thing.

I'm off, racing toward school, racing toward a better start to the day, racing toward the love of my life, who I hope is still waiting at our meeting spot.

Huffing and puffing, I arrive at the lunch area and slump onto a bench. I hunch over the table, sucking in air. Breathe in. Breathe out. I lift my weary head. No Josh. Wah.

But waltzing toward me is Candy, an eighth grader sprinkled with what looks like an entire truckload of glitter. I can't even imagine why she's here. Everyone hangs out at the front of the school. Which is why Josh and I chose the lunch tables. For privacy.

Candy says, "You lookin' for Josh Morton?"

I nod, my breathing still all kicked up and cardio.

She juts her hip out to, like, Tucson. "He didn't wait for you."

"What?" My heart folds in half as I push off the table and stand.

"Good thing I was here for him."

I roll my eyes. No way Josh is interested in Glitter Girl. I'm right, right? I stick my hand in my pocket and finger the teeny card that came with the flowers. I'm right.

"We're doing an English project together."

Big whopping deal. It's an English project, not a date.

Candy's totally focused on my face. "You might want to outline your lips before glossing. So they don't look as thin."

My hand jumps to my mouth. No one's ever mentioned my lips and thin in the same sentence before. Then again, how credible is an overglittered girl with a ratty ponytail and a skirt the size of my math textbook?

"Anyway, Josh picked me as his partner. Specifically." She swings out her other hip to, like, Flagstaff.

Yada yada yada. Everything's totally awesome between Josh and me. Well, okay, it hasn't been so intense lately. But that's 'cause he's juggling school and water polo and helping his dad out with the family landscaping business.

11

Suddenly, Candy is slanted way forward and stumbling toward the restroom. She throws her arms out, plants her feet on the pavement and bends her knees. It's like she's fighting against an invisible force.

I sniff the air. Yuppers. It's coffee. My mother has landed.

Baby step by baby step, Mom pushes Candy. Glitter sparkles in the air, floating on the breeze. Finally, Candy lurches across the threshold and into the restroom.

"It looked like she was giving you a hard time." Mom's next to me now, sounding all proud of herself.

"Well, yeah, she was," I say. "Thanks."

"Oh, Sherry"—Mom's voice bubbles—"my skills are improving by leaps and bounds. Did you see how I got here all on my own, without your grandfather? And how I directed all my energy at that girl?" The metal bench creaks as my mom settles in.

"Wow, Mom, that's great." I give a little shake at the thought of all this weirdness in my life. Still, weirdness beats no contact with my mother. Some days, I just wish we could chill and get our nails done together or something else mother-daughter normal. But that can't happen.

The first bell rings. I stand, swinging my backpack over my shoulder. "Nice to see you, Mom."

She clears her throat. "Sherry, I'm here for a reason."

This doesn't sound good. "What?"

Her words rush out. "We have an appointment with my guidance counselor today at noon."

Both of us? At noon? That's when Josh and I have lunch. When I'll find out what he wants to tell me. "Noon doesn't really work for me."

"It was an order. Apparently we need to discuss something 'personal.' "

"Personal? Your personal? Or my personal? Because I can't think of anything personal to do with me that needs to be discussed with a ghost guidance counselor. So it must be your personal. Which means I don't have to be there at all."

"The message said both of us, Sherry. And, believe me, you do not want to tangle with my guidance counselor."

A breeze gusts through the lunch area. "Be at the Dairy Queen. In the back booth. At noon." My mother's voice fades as she's blown away. She's still having trouble hanging on to locations.

I plod across campus. Not having a fun day here. No Josh time before school. A bummer run-in with Glitter Girl, who's obviously after my boyfriend. A lunchtime meeting with a mean ghost guidance counselor. Nope. Definitely not enjoying this fine Friday.

I shove my hands in my pockets, and my right hand closes around the card from the flowers.

The second bell rings.

Second bell, schmecond bell. I deserve a romance pick-me-up. I stop walking. With my thumb and index finger, I gently tug on the tiny flap of the envelope and slide out the card. My heart pitter-pattering with love, I gaze down and read.

chapter
three

Swoon. Swoon. Swoon. I clutch the card to my chest.

A few minutes later, I'm jostling into line at the computer lab door.

Ahead of me, Honor Roll Girl says to Tongue-Stud Girl, "The Ruler's giving us the next project today. I can't wait to get started." And she's not even being sarcastic.

Next project? The last one nearly killed me, as in a big, plump C. I positively must ace this one or I'll have to deal with The Ruler's extra help again.

Also, have these middle-grade teachers never heard of communication? Why pile on a bunch of work all at the same time? We have a massive science test next week. And a French vocab quiz. And really hard homework. I want a life!

The bell rings.

Nerdy Nick says to me, "Think your friend'll make it on time?"

I don't answer him. It's my new strategy. Since the beginning of the school year, when Nerdy Nick and his entire nerdy family moved here, I've put up with his uncalled-for comments about my half-finished homework and less-than-stellar grades. I tried being nice. I tried being funny. Now I'm trying frosty.

I look over my shoulder. Jogging along the pathway is my best friend, Junie Carter. Hair flying out behind her and shirt all crooked, she's hunched forward with the effort of running. Junie is the opposite of athletic. But she's the definition of smart.

The classroom door opens and The Ruler says, "File in quietly and take your seats quickly. We have a lot to cover."

Junie brakes to a stop, a shoe length away from crashing into me. "My dad had to get gas this morning." With the back of her hand, she brushes hair off her sweaty forehead. "Come on." She hitches up her backpack. "Let's go in. She's giving out the new assignment today."

I shove the card at her. "Josh left flowers on the porch. It's our two-month anniversary."

"Very cool." She glances down at the card. " 'Happy

Anniversary!'" she reads aloud. "And a peace sign? He doesn't even sign his name?"

"'Cause we're so tight." Junie's not interested in guys, so there's a lot to do with dating, et cetera, that she doesn't get yet. Although I have to admit, the peace sign is something new.

"Junie. Sherry. Move along." The Ruler's at the door, herding us in.

Junie hands me back the card.

The Ruler glances at it. She flushes. What's her problem anyway? It's not officially class time yet.

Junie and I scoot into back-row seats, adding to the general classroom noise of scraping chair legs, sliding metal zippers and rustling papers. This is the first week we haven't had assigned seating. And I'm loving it.

Arms crossed and feet shoulder-width apart, The Ruler stands guard, making sure we're all settling down. Once she's satisfied we're paying attention, she flips open her laptop.

"Let's talk about your next assignment." She punches the On button. "This is the perfect opportunity for any of you who need to recover from a low grade on the 'Hello, World' project." She walks over to the wall and dims the lights. While the computer boots up, she's spouting all kinds of computery mumbo jumbo.

I yawn. Another one of The Ruler's boring PowerPoint

presentations. I slowly ease my phone from my pocket and thumb-type a text to Junie: <mom & me have mtg at noon with her counselor> I've barely pressed Send when a skinny shadow darkens my desk. The Ruler hawk-swoops down, grabs my cell with her talons, soars to her desk, slides open a drawer and drops in my precious phone. Which I won't get back till the end of the day. School rules.

Nerdy Nick wags his finger and silently tsk-tsks me.

Junie's scribbling in her notebook. Then she reaches into her pocket and pulls out her cell. My message has arrived. She eyeballs it and goes back to writing. When The Ruler's totally into answering a suck-up question from Honor Roll Girl, Junie mouths at me, "Another mystery?"

I shrug.

Technically, Junie shouldn't even know about my mother or the Academy. But I had this one really bad day, when I was totally overwhelmed by life, and I spilled.

The good news is, Junie can help with investigations. The bad news is, Mom's extremely talented ghost study group can't. All because the Academy uses this crazy Weight-Watchers-ish point system to figure out how much support the spiritual students get. And Junie, being human, uses up too many points. Like she's a double-double cheeseburger meal with a shake at In-N-Out Burger.

The Ruler's clicking on her mouse and droning in a language that sounds like English but makes no sense. "Blah, blah, blah, pull, blah, blah, stack, blah, algorithm."

The remainder of the class goes by in a blur. Let's face it: the entire class went by in a blur. Which is totally understandable. I have a lot on my mind: Josh, Candy, freakish lips, lunchtime Dairy Queen meeting.

After the bell, I join a wave of students moving along the walkway. Junie stays behind to ask questions about the project. So I'm bobbing across campus and mentally scrolling through Josh's classes, a schedule I know better than the periodic table. Next he has social studies, which means he's going from English to social studies, which means he'll cross the courtyard, which means if I hang out near the tall, ugly, stone saguaro cactus statue, he'll pass by me.

Snippets of conversation manage to pierce through my calculations.

Tongue-Stud Girl says, "There's a robotics club meeting today, right?"

"In the shop room," Honor Roll Girl says. "We better get on top of things if we're going to kill Donner Middle School again this year."

"I heard they're out to get us," Tongue-Stud Girl says. " 'Cause we made it to the world championships last year. And they didn't."

Nerdy Nick says, "They better get used to the idea."

Last year was the first time The Ruler took over the club. It was also the first time that Saguaro beat Donner. Donner's been making it to the championships in Atlanta for, like, ever. But so yesterday's news.

"Are you joining, Sherry?" Honor Roll Girl swings her backpack to her other shoulder. "You'd be a real asset."

Me? A real asset to the robotics club? Doing what? Bringing snacks?

"She has a C in computer," Nerdy Nick says. "Quit trying to recruit everyone, Meghan."

Honor Roll Girl jumps away from me like I've got a rash.

"Sherry!" a male voice calls.

The voice lightning-bolts straight down my spine.

I gaze around and spot Josh.

My legs go all rubbery, like when you're forced to run the mile the first week in PE, and you haven't done one millisecond of exercise over the summer.

He's leaning against the cactus statue, the sun lighting him up like he's on a stage. His shaggy hair glints, throwing off extra sparks where the pool water has bleached it from light brown to blond. He's wearing my favorite T-shirt, Totally Tones, that's the exact same blue as his gorgeous eyes. And his Dickies jeans sag at the perfect angle off his hips. Sigh.

When I get close, Josh pulls me in for a hug. I inhale. It's that Josh smell: laundry soap from his clothes mixed with chlorine from the pool.

We break apart.

"Missed you this morning," he says. "What happened?"

"What happened was The Ruler. I had to help her find her keys."

"Drag."

"Definite drag."

"I wanted to talk to you about tonight," Josh says. "Well, this afternoon and toni—"

"Wait a sec," I interrupt him. "Where were *you*? I got to the lunch tables before the bell."

He looks surprised. "Didn't Candy tell you?"

I cross my arms. "Tell me what?"

"About Magee."

I squeeze my biceps. Well, where my biceps would be if I had any.

"Yesterday in class, Magee told me I needed to do my *The Call of the Wild* presentation with a strong student 'cause my English grade sucks." Josh hitches up his jeans. They immediately slide back down. "So when he saw me talking to Candy this morning while I was waiting for you, he said she didn't have a partner yet and we should work together."

"I still don't get why you weren't there."

"Magee made me follow him to his office to get

some papers. Candy said she'd wait behind to tell you." He shoves his hands in his pocket. "Guess something came up, and she left."

Candy is so dead meat. Trying to make me think Josh doesn't like me anymore. "Do you have to work with her?"

"Seems like I better. Magee said it would raise my grade." With his palm, Josh tips up my chin and looks straight at me. "You're not jealous of Candy Lopez, are you?"

"Uh, no," I say loudly.

"Hey"—his smile crinkles up his eyes and makes him look even more adorable—"wait'll you hear my plans for later."

I go all still.

"There's a water polo scrimmage at Donner after school. Can you get a ride? I have to take the bus." He's talking fast, all excited. "My mom has time between clients. So after the game, she can pick us up at Donner and drive us somewhere for dinner. Sit-down, not takeout. For our three-month anniversary."

"Two. Two-month." I throw my arms around his neck. "Josh Morton, you're the best."

He hugs me back. "No argument here." He steps away and pulls out his cell to check the time. "I gotta get to—"

"Social studies," I finish for him. "And I gotta get to . . ."

Josh scrunches up his forehead, thinking. "Computer?"

"Science," I say, all fake exasperated, pretending to be shockerooed he doesn't know.

"Josh Man!" Eric, Josh's best friend, calls from across the quad. "Wait up!" They have social studies together. Eric skids in, shoelaces dragging, and punches Josh in the arm. "Guess what, man? I'm going to the scrimmage." He glances at me. "Hi, Sherry."

I baby-wave. I would love it if Junie and Eric got together. Talk about your awesome double-dating possibilities. Sadly, both Junie and Eric have ignored my romance hints.

Josh punches Eric back. "Cool." He plants a quick kiss on my cheek. "Catch ya at lunch."

Those water polo guys are fast movers—Josh and Eric take off before I have a chance to mention I won't be around at lunch. Probably just as well. Because secrecy is a major Academy rule, Josh can't know about my mother. His speedy exit prevents me from having to make up a lame excuse.

I slap my forehead with the heel of my hand. I just remembered what I forgot to say to him.

chapter
four

Dairy Queen, Phoenix, Arizona. Aka the main campus of the Academy of Spirits, according to my mother. Apparently, there's a satellite campus in Canada somewhere. Probably in an igloo.

Gripping the handle till my knuckles go white, I stand at the glass door. I am so not ready for this creepy, freaky, ghostly experience.

I stare into the restaurant. At least DQ's not too crowded. Just a few construction guys ordering at the counter and a very pregnant woman zoned out in front of a giant Oreo Brownie Earthquake poster. I count to ten to get my courage up, then yank the door open and step in.

An arctic blast from the air-conditioning smacks

me in the face. I sniff for coffee to see if my mother's around. Negative. Nothing but a heavy, syrupy, ice creamy smell.

I round the corner, heading for the famous back booth. I slide in and wait, legs stretched out, ankles crossed.

With a sudden gust of coffee scent, Mom says in my ear, "Not this booth. The other back booth."

I look around in confusion. "What other back booth?"

"Through the door. Follow me."

"I can't go there. It says Employees Only."

"Hurry, Sherry. Mrs. Howard doesn't tolerate lateness."

With puffs of wind, she hustles me forward till I'm squished up against the door. I shoulder it open and step across the threshold.

Zap! Zap! Zap!

"Ouch! Ouch! Ouch!"

Zillions of teeny sparks zing and ping me. I'm trapped in some sort of *Star Trek* force field.

"Mom! Mom! Mom!"

"Keep walking, Sherry," my mother says.

I stumble out of the portal of pain and slump to the floor. Every inch of my skin tingles and itches. "I'm injured. I'm injured," I groan.

There's a feathery fluttering as my mother moves across me, checking me out.

"You're fine. Your hair's just a little messy."

I put a hand up to my head.

Ack. Eek. Ike.

My hair, if I can still call it that, bounces and springs back against my palm. It's like a giant bird's nest after a violent windstorm. I doubt even gallons of pricey salon conditioner will calm it down. I'll probably end up getting a buzz cut and starting from scratch. And I don't think Josh dates bald girls. Certainly Candy has hair.

"My—my hair," I stammer, "my hair."

"It's not that bad, Sherry," my mom says. "Stand up. She'll be here any minute."

My mother is not known for her sympathy. With a minimum of moaning, I pull myself to my feet. While reclipping my frizz, I gaze around. I'm in front of a booth identical to the one on the other side of the door. Well, almost identical. A Blizzard sits in the middle of the Formica table.

"It's for you," Mom says. The tall cup scoots toward me. "Oreo Cookie."

"Wow. Thanks." Oreo Cookie's my fave.

"It was Mrs. Howard's idea."

I scoop up a spoonful. "I thought you said she was mean."

"Shhh. And I didn't call her mean. I just said you don't want to tangle with her."

The words are no sooner out of her mouth than the booth swells with the smell of cinnamon rolls. Fresh, warm dough, melted sugar, lots of cinnamon. It's like I'm in the Cinnabon store at the mall. Only yummier.

I raise my shoulders and inhale deeply. Like a cat, I arch into the back of the bench, my spine xylophoning along the slats while the tension of the day slowly drains out of me. I'm totally chill and mellow. Cinnamon rolls do that to me. And Mrs. Howard smells like a cinnamon roll.

Wait a sec! I'm actually smelling a ghost other than my mother. That's never happened before.

The bench across from me creaks and shifts.

I squint. Wow! I can make out a faint shape. A faint overweight, short, snowballish shape. I can very vaguely see Mrs. Howard. I wonder if it'll be like that with my mother once she's advanced through a bunch of Academy levels. What if one day I could actually see my mom? My throat goes all hard-to-swallow.

"Howdy, y'all," a female voice says, the vowels stretched out and drowsy.

"Hi, Minnie May." My mom sounds tense, her words crisp and clipped.

"Sherry, honey, I am so glad to finally make your acquaintance. I'm Mrs. Howard."

Her voice is musical and friendly, full of kindness and hospitality. I can just imagine how in real life, she'd fold me up in a big, squishy, cinnamony hug. She is so not mean. Obviously, my mother is a lousy judge of character.

I smile. "Nice to meet you too." I scoop up a spoon-ful of Blizzard. It melts into a tiny ice creamy puddle on my tongue.

"I want to thank you, Sherry, for taking time for us from your school day. Here at the Academy, we all admire your talent for juggling an active teen life and our spiritual business."

Loving this Mrs. Howard. She so gets me.

"Sherry, honey, here's a little something to make it easier when you need to summon your mama."

A ziplock bag drifts lazily down from the ceiling, landing lightly on the table in front of me.

Mrs. Howard says, "Arabica espresso beans. From Costa Rica. Easier to handle than a cup of coffee."

Coffee is what I use to call my mother. It's a beverage I can't stand the taste of.

I have spilled way too many cups of java, ruining way too many cute outfits. So, coffee beans? That's rocking. "Wow. Very cool. Thanks."

Mrs. Howard's fuzzy head nods. "Okay, girls, time for y'all to get serious," she drawls.

A hologram of a plasma screen appears on the wall. It's blank for a moment with Halloweenish, bad-guy organ music playing in the background.

Uh-oh. Up on the screen is a head shot of me. I can't help but notice it was taken on a good hair day. I'm sitting on my bed, smiling and yakking on my cell. The screen splits. On the left half, The Ruler, in an apron, is calling me from the bottom of the stairs. On the right half, I frown but keep talking on the phone. She calls me again. I ignore her again. She calls me again. I still ignore her. She runs into the kitchen, turns off the burner where her spicy tomato sauce is bubbling away, trudges up the stairs and pokes her head into my room. I roll my eyes and snap my cell shut. Your basic teen attitude. But supersized.

My chest is squeezed tight like I'm wearing a rubber band shirt. How embarrassing to have my meanness captured on film.

A couple more scenes of me being rude to The Ruler and the screen goes blank, then disappears. Finally.

The delish Cinnabon smell has been replaced by burnt sugar.

"The Academy's mission is to watch over and protect humans." Mrs. Howard's voice is all sharp and disciplining. "As of this moment, Sherry, the disrespect stops. Or you'll lose the privilege of helping your mama."

I gulp in some air. Shallow, fishlike breaths 'cause of the rubber band feeling.

"Now, let me brief you about your next case," Mrs. Howard continues. "It involves Paula."

The Ruler? I feel my eyes go round as water polo balls.

"She has a stalker," Mrs. Howard says. "Y'all's assignment is to identify the stalker and deliver him or her to the authorities. Do not, I repeat, do not let anything happen to Paula."

"Is she aware she has a stalker?" Presto. My mother transforms into investigative mode.

"No, she is not," Mrs. Howard says.

"How do you know it's a stalker?" I ask. "And not just an annoyed student?" One of many, I think, but keep the thought to myself.

Mrs. Howard turns her blurry balloonish head toward me. "Because I trust the judgment of the Phantom Security Squad, the PSS. They're a talented, experienced Academy department responsible for investigating misdemeanors against humans. If they're convinced Paula has a stalker, I'm convinced Paula has a stalker."

"What else does the PSS say?" Mom asks.

"They believe this to be a run-of-the-mill mystery," Mrs. Howard replies. "We at the Academy expect that you ladies will be able to solve the case, all the while improving your relationship with Paula."

Does the fun never end?

"By the way, I'll personally be checking up on y'all. Making sure your behavior's aboveboard." With a loud rustle, like someone gathering up her petticoats, the roundish shape rises. "Because Paula and I are kin. We share a great-great-great granddaddy, which makes me Paula's great-great-aunt. And we Southerners always look after our own."

chapter
five

Mom flies beside me while I hoof it back to school. "Sherry, Paula's doing all those things for you and Sam and Dad that I can't. Driving you to appointments, making sure homework is done, cooking, cleaning. The list goes on," she says. "She really cares for you guys. We're lucky to have her."

"Yeah, I know." I sigh. "But I just want you. I want the old days back."

"Me too, me too," Mom says softly. "But that's not going to happen. And you can't take it out on Paula."

I sigh again. "We better make sure we catch the stalker."

"Got any ideas on where to start?"

"There's a staff meeting after classes today," I say.

"Great!" Mom's all over an investigation. "I'll eavesdrop to get a sense of how the staff feels about Paula. The stalker could be one of them."

At the edge of school property, I stop and rub the toe of my ballet slipper on the curb. Saguaro Middle School is a closed campus, which means you're not allowed off the grounds during the day. Unless a parent signs you out for an ortho appointment or whatever. So leaving and getting back to class can be kind of tricky. And kind of a fun challenge.

"I'll go on my own from here," I say.

Mom laughs. "You were always good at hide-and-seek."

I wend my way through the school parking lot, crouching down low between cars. A quick dash puts me by the foreign languages classrooms. I round the corner and screech to a halt.

Yikes. It's Ms. Ortiz, the vice principal. All Nancy Drewish, I tiptoe back to the side of the building, flatten myself and wait, barely breathing.

Ms. Ortiz gazes around, then heads toward the office. The second she's out of sight, I beeline it to French.

Just as Madame Blanchard's closing the door, I squeeze through.

Le français is not my thing; I'm generally clueless about what's going on in there, but it's still the best period of the day. Madame Blanchard, aka Madame

Babblepants, has zero control over the class. Translation: I can always catch up on the daily gossip, indulge in some creative doodling and, my fave activity, daydream about Josh.

The desks are pushed together in pairs. I usually don't sit with Junie, who takes French way too seriously. But today I make an exception; I've gotta get her take on the stalker business.

"*Comment ça va?*" Junie asks.

"*Je m'appelle* Sherry," I answer, sliding into the seat next to her.

"I asked how you're doing, not what your name is." Junie rolls her eyes.

"Puhleeze. You asked in French. I answered in French." I roll my eyes back at her. "Works for me."

"How crazy was the meeting with your mom and her guidance counselor?"

"Beyond crazy." I tell her about the Cinnabon-scented, Southern-speaking Mrs. Howard with her Blizzard gift, espresso beans and evil hologram screen. "And guess what? Mom and I have a new assignment. Apparently, The Ruler has a stalker."

Junie's somewhat bushy eyebrows shoot up in surprise. "Really?"

"I know, I know. El shockeroo. Have you seen anything that would make you think she does? Because I haven't." I scoot my backpack under the desk, cross my ankles and rest my feet on it. "Is The Ruler bizarre? Yes. Annoying? Yes. Old? Yes. Stalked? News to me."

Junie's tongue pokes out between her teeth, a sign she's thinking hard. "She's been pretty clumsy lately. Like in math this morning? She could not hold on to the pointer to save her life." Junie lines up a pen and a highlighter. "She's been ditzy too. In robotics club the other day, she was hunting in the tool chest for motion sensors. You know what those are, right? For the front and back of our robot, so if it bumps into something—"

"Earth to Junie. It's me you're talking to." I make hurry-up-and-spit-it-out circles with my hand. "Ixnay on the details."

She frowns. "The Ruler was looking for some things. She couldn't find them. When I looked, there were a bunch of them. Right in view, on top of some other things." She looks at me, her eyebrows raised. "That explanation work for you?"

"Absolutely. Nice and simple."

Junie butts her special stripy notebook for her French notes up against the pen and highlighter on her desk. "Maybe the stuff with the pointer and the motion sensors is a sign that she's worried about having a stalker?"

"Nah," I say. "She doesn't even know she has one. She's just mega overextended. What with teaching and my dad gone and robotics." Hands above my head, I squeeze my hair clip. "Like, she's normally so fanatical about housework with all-natural products and lots of cleaning and dusting and HEPA-filter vacuuming. But I've noticed our place doesn't smell too good lately. And, she lost her keys again this a.m."

"Yeah, well, this *is* our busiest time in robotics." Junie pulls a paperback French-English dictionary from her backpack. "We're almost at the end of the six weeks allotted to build our bot and test it out at the practice competition. The whole team is frazzled."

Someone needs a major reality check. "Frazzled" and "robotics club" so don't go together.

At the front of the class, Madame Babblepants begins her daily nonsensical, uh, babble.

"Hmmm," Junie mumbles at me, her eyes all focused on Madame, who's handing Nerdy Nick a stack of worksheets to pass out.

Flinging a couple on my desk, Nerdy Nick says, "Hey, Sherry, wanna save us all some time?" He picks up Junie's pen and marks a big F at the top of my first paper.

In a smooth move, Junie reaches out a hand for her pen and transforms the F into an A. "Be nice, Nick."

Miracle of miracles, he actually goes red and mumbles, "Sorry, Sherry."

Who knew Junie had such power?

In the meantime, Junie's hunched over her desk, diving into verb conjugations. Like they're peanut butter and jelly, you cannot separate Junie from her 4.0.

We've been best friends for ages, ever since beginner swimming, even though we're pretty much polar opposites. Junie's brilliant and into school, like an engineer or something. I'm social and fashionable and into boys. With such different talents, we can really help each other out.

I watch her for a second while she messes with the verb *conduire*. From the cartoon picture of a car on the worksheet, I'm guessing it means "to drive." I watch Junie's pen fly over the page, drawing lines to match up *je conduis* with "I drive" and *tu conduis* with "you drive." When she hits *nous conduisons*/we drive, I figure out where I'm headed next, mysterywise.

chapter
six

After last period, I trudge across campus to The Ruler's classroom.

Honor Roll Girl is standing next to The Ruler's desk. "I just want to be sure I understand how to get extra credit on the assignment, Ms. Paulson."

After marrying my dad a couple of months ago, The Ruler didn't change her name at school. Phew for me. There's gotta be a couple of students hidden under a rock on campus who don't know The Ruler's my stepmom.

All serious and professional, The Ruler gives Honor Roll Girl a few pointers, then says, "Good enough, Meghan?"

"Well," Honor Roll Girl says, getting ready to launch into more sucking-up mode.

"Why don't you start setting up for robotics in the shop room? You'll be taking on a leadership role today while I'm at the staff meeting."

Honor Roll Girl literally puffs out her chest with pride and struts to the door. Yikes.

The Ruler opens the top desk drawer and pulls out my phone. She hands it to me.

One good thing about The Ruler is she doesn't nag. I broke the cell phone rule; she punished me; I got my cell back; end of story. No long, boring lecture.

I stick my phone in the side pocket of my backpack, waiting till the door closes behind Honor Roll Girl. Then I say, "Can you give me a ride to Donner? For the water polo game?" So much for my personal rule of not getting into The Ruler's hybrid on campus.

Her eyes widen. Just a teeny-tiny bit because she's pretty much always in control. But she's surprised 'cause I don't ask her for too many favors, especially at school. "Sure, Sherry. When?"

"Uh, now?" Even though it's last minute, she'll do her best to help me out. I can always count on her that way.

The Ruler glances at the wall clock and nods. "I can just squeeze it in before the staff meeting." She turns off her computer. "How will you get home?"

"Josh's mom. She's driving us to a restaurant first

for dinner. And I don't have to worry about home-work 'cause it's Friday."

"Sounds like you've got the evening organized. Good job." The Ruler grabs a pile of papers off her desk and slides them into a file drawer. She throws her purse over her shoulder. "Let's go."

We ride along mostly in silence. The Ruler's an incredibly cautious driver. Seat totally upright and shoulders stiff and tense like she's a statue in a wax museum, she concentrates on signaling and switching lanes.

Stopped at a red light, she says, "Do you know where you're going for dinner?"

"Just that it's a sit-down restaurant, not fast food."

A smile tugs at her lips, but she doesn't say anything more until she's driving on a straight road with no other vehicles around. "I like the way Josh treats you, Sherry."

"I know. He's so legit." Once I start gushing about Josh, I could go on for miles. "And he even got me flowers for our anniversary today. With a cute, adorable mini card. Oh yeah, you saw the card in class. Anyway, total surprise. I tripped over them on the porch this morning. I left them there 'cause I was running late. Do you think they're okay? Not wilted or dead?"

"No, they're fine. I saw them and put them in a vase." Her face flushes like it did at the beginning of class.

Why would me getting flowers turn her red? Adults can be so bizarro. I think kids growing up kinda freaks them out.

The Ruler eases into a visitor spot and nudges the car into park. "You know where you're going on campus?"

"No, I've never been here before. But it's a water polo game; I'll follow the whistles to the pool." I unbuckle and push open the passenger door. "So, uh, you know, be careful." I can't bring myself to say, "Hey, watch your back: you've got a stalker." Because it sounds way, way out there.

"You too, Sherry."

After The Ruler noses away, I stand on the sidewalk and listen for whistle blasts. Nada. The teams must still be warming up. I start along the main sidewalk leading onto campus.

It's quiet; I'm not passing any students or teachers. I meander along, one ear cocked for whistle blasts and one eye peeled for a restroom, because, now that I'm aware of my below-average-lips situation, I'm doing multiple major gloss touch-ups. To create an illusion of plumpness.

I'm so busy listening for whistles and watching for restrooms that I practically walk smack into a pole. A pole with a white poster on it. A white poster with a turquoise-ish arrow.

I'm at a fork in the path, and the arrow points to

the right. I look up and read the black-markered
message on the poster:

```
        ! ! DONNER DYNAMOS
     ROBOTICS CLUB MEETING! !
          TODAY @ 4:00 P.M.
        IN THE COMPUTER LAB
   THIS YEAR WE DESTROY THE SAGUARO
             CACTI AND
      BRING HOME OUR TROPHY! !
         JOIN AND BE PART
        OF DONNER HISTORY! !
          WE NEED YOU! !
      YUMMY SNACKS AT MEETING! !
```

Tongue-Stud Girl's words from this morning echo
in my mind. About how Donner's out to get us 'cause
we dominated them last year. Oh, puhleeze. No one
in their right mind would be so into robotics that
they'd stalk the teacher of a rival team. Why would
you bother? What would be the point?

A whistle rips through the air. From the left path.

I stare at the poster. "Destroy" is a pretty strong
word. Another whistle blast.

Water polo to the left. Robotics to the right. Isn't
there a poem about this? Not about this exactly, but
about having to choose a path. And Nerdy Nick
thinks I never pay attention in class. Ha!

What if I went to the robotics meeting for five fleeting minutes? In five minutes, I could rule out the Donner Dynamos as an all-star team of stalkers. I could report to my mom that I already started investigating. I could nosh on some snacks. And then I could head poolside to see Josh. . . .

More whistles and a buzzer. My cute ballet slippers slapping the pavement, I jog off in the direction of the arrow. At the computer room door, there's a long-faced, short-haired stubby guy in an overly wrinkled button-down shirt. A flash drive dangles from a lanyard around his neck.

"You coming in here?" he says, his hand on the door handle.

I nod.

He releases the handle and steps toward me. "You'll be our tenth and final member." He's swinging his flash drive like it's some kind of neck metronome. The faster he swings, the faster he talks. "We're gearing up for the practice competition. And then, like for all the teams, our bot is crated and sent to storage so that we only see it for competitions. Claire has a bunch of stuff she wants us to tackle today."

I take a step back. I don't want the swinging flash drive to connect with my skull. Plus, the guy's standing just a little too close. In fact, he's just a little too friendly. And a little too enthusiastic. I mean, we're talking robotics here. Not something truly exciting like clothes or makeup or teen magazines.

Flash Drive Guy finally stops for a breath, and I break in. "So Claire's the teacher-mentor for your club?"

"No. No. No. Claire's an eighth grader. Our president. She's brilliant." *Swing. Swing. Swing.* "Although she does put the 'boss' in 'bossy.' But she grows on you." *Swing. Swing. Swing.* "How can you not know any of this? What planet are you from?"

"The Planet of Homeschooling." Talk about your very brilliant response. Because how suspicious would that look if I didn't have a single class with a single person in the club?

"I'm Austin." He whips open the door. "Come in and meet the gang." He slides in ahead of me and announces, "New person. She's homeschooled."

Eight people sit or kneel on a big blue tarp. They're surrounded by springs and wheels and loads of other brain-puzzle bits and pieces. A girl's plugging in a drill. Several toolboxes lean against the wall behind the students.

Austin yanks open a toolbox drawer and tosses me and everybody else a pair of safety glasses. They do not match my outfit. Actually, oversized plastic safety glasses don't match anybody's outfit.

A girl with dyed midnight black hair, chin length on

one side, shoulder length on the other, stares at me. Practically stares through me. Her lips are perfectly plump and shimmer with peach gloss that complements her baby-doll top.

When you're a detective, you notice details. When you're a fashion queen, like myself, you notice even more.

"Claire?" I ask.

She pulls herself slowly to a stand, swaying like a cobra. "Yeah. And you are?"

"I'm, uh, uh, homeschooled." Yikes. My mind blanked. I can't believe I forgot to think of a fake name.

"She means, what's your name?" Austin says.

Thank you, Austin, who I'm sure has many friends, given his helpful personality. I tap my thinnish bottom lip. Sherry. Sherry. Rhymes with . . . "Mary."

"We don't usually let homeschooled kids join our team." Claire hooks hair from the longer side behind her ear.

"You have to let me. It's the law." Here is an advantage of living with The Ruler, who has mentioned at the dinner table how public schools must allow homeschooled kids to join extracurricular clubs. I know for sure we have a couple in the band at Saguaro.

Claire hooks hair from the shorter side behind her ear. "Mary, got any experience with robots?"

"Some." If you count babysitting a younger brother who plays with Transformers. "I know about motion sensors." If you count having a best friend who plays with them.

Like they're waking up from a deep sleep, the other students start adding to the conversation. They obviously all bow to Queen Claire, though. A girl in cool boots says, "We could use some extra help." A guy with a mohawk says, "The practice competition is just around the corner."

"Come on, Bryce," Austin says to a redheaded guy who's kneeling and sorting miniature thingies into piles by shape. Very *Sesame Street*.

They go into a small room at the back and return with a piece of plywood on wheels. In the middle of this homemade dolly sits a big lump hidden under a thick blanket. They wheel the dolly onto the tarp.

Then, pulling on a corner of the blanket, Claire begins to slowly unveil the lump. With a final yank, it's revealed.

Squatting on the plywood is a gray metal platform about the size of a kitchen tray. Attached to it are smaller gray metal rectangular pieces, a few gray metal stick arms, rubber wheels and many, many unsightly wires. It's about knee high.

Sometimes, a thought from my brain will gallop out of my mouth before I can lasso it. I say, "That's your robot? Could it be more boring?"

Shocked silence in the Donner computer lab.

Another thought gallops out. "You need to seriously bling out this robot. So it looks totally different from every other robot at the competitions." I walk over to the dolly and examine the robot from all angles. "Are your school colors white, black and turquoise?"

A girl with a bunch of forehead pimples says, "Yeah."

"I've got some gorgeous glass gemstones and sequins left over from decorating my bedroom that we could use. They're turquoise plus sea green, a cuter color than just plain turquoise." I launch into a description of my room and aquarium, because the two totally coordinate. It's the way my fish and I roll. For my walls, I mixed up this unique turquoise + sea green paint at Home Depot and tossed in glitter. I sewed sequins in different shapes on my beautiful wavy blue and green bedspread. I glued glass gemstones around the doorframe and windowsill. I painted and decorated mini castles and treasure chests for my fish. And finally, after months and months of hunting, I found turquoise + sea green gravel for the bottom of the tank. Quite frankly, my room and aquarium could be featured in a fancy-schmancy decorating magazine. Or at least in a pet magazine.

Okay. No need for me to help the Donner team. But

when it comes to beauty and fashion, even for a robot, I'm all about sharing. It's my generous nature.

Claire rudely interrupts my chat. "Button people? Can you use Mary?"

"Not really; we're in good shape," Mohawk Guy says. "We're making buttons with our logo to hand out at the meets," he explains to me. "All the teams do."

"Website people?" Claire barks. "Can you use Mary?"

Pimply Forehead Girl raises her hand.

Claire frowns. "You don't have to put your hand up, Sarah."

"Oh, yeah, right." Sarah slams her arm down to her lap. "I really like the bling idea."

A lot of kids, even boys, are nodding.

"Mary's right." All excited, Austin bounces on the balls of his feet. "We should individualize our robot."

"Fine. Bring in your junk," Claire says.

I think she's secretly thrilled with the bling thing; she didn't argue against it. She probably doesn't want to show her enthusiasm because it wasn't her idea.

"Back to the website people." Claire's chewing on her nails. "Do you want Mary?"

Sarah gets her hand partially up before jamming it in her pocket. "We'll take her for Web interviews." She says to me, "We get points for our website. We still haven't done our team interviews. It's where we collect info about each member and upload it to our site. We need someone to take over that. Like develop a questionnaire, type in our answers."

I could handle that. In fact, I'd rock at that. I'm really talented at getting people to talk about themselves. Donner would have the best interviews in the contest.

Wait! I'm not actually joining the Donner robotics club. I'm not really homeschooled. My name is Sherry, not Mary.

Claire says, "Interviews are good for Mary."

"How about plan A?" Austin asks. "We could use her there."

They're fighting over me. I love it.

Claire shuts him down with a look.

"What's plan A?" I say. "I'm probably down with plan A. Or B?" Very *Cat in the Hat*.

"How do you know about plan B?" Claire bites the words off through clenched teeth.

"Uh, I don't? I was referring to *The Cat in the Hat* with all the little cats and their plans to get rid of the pink?" I roll my eyes. "Don't you people read?"

"You're on interviews." Claire turns to the bot. "People, we're still having probs with the limit switch for the claw. We need the claw to open and close more smoothly if we're going to pick up and deposit rings."

I wander around looking for the yummy snacks. Sadly, I am finding nothing, not even one single stale pretzel. I'm obviously the victim of false advertising.

Yikes. I can't believe I didn't notice it before, but this computer lab stinks. Like the PE locker room at school. The boys' PE locker room. Don't even ask me how I know. So is the Donner custodial staff a bunch of slackers? There's a faint sweet smell too, like they sprayed cheap air freshener instead of actually cleaning. Honey + dirty socks is not a winning combination.

Plugging my nose, I walk over to the window and start opening it.

A group gasp gusts through the room.

"What do you think you're doing?" Claire's right beside me, hands on the sill, pushing down. Her black fingernails glisten next to my light pink ones. "We don't open windows here. You're not in your own home, Homeschool Girl."

"Aren't you worried about losing brain cells from the smell?" I say.

"What?" And she genuinely looks confused.

The others do too.

Obviously it's too late for them. Their brain cells are already fried.

"Sarah, get her started on the interview stuff," Claire says and shoots me one last you're-insane look.

"Yeah, we don't want any lame Saguaro Cacti kinds of questions." A bunch of the students cackle.

49

For the first time in my life, I feel the urge to stick up for my school's robotics team. I could so kick Bryce's piles of junk across the room. Instead, I say, "What's the deal with Saguaro?"

"We're going to pulverize them this year," Mohawk Guy says.

"They stole the trophy from us last year," Sarah explains.

"All because of Paulson. They were never any good before her." Bryce punctuates his statement by opening his fist and dropping a handful of doohickeys into a bucket.

Alternating palms, Austin hits the tarp and chants, "Donner. Dynamos. Donner. Dynamos." Very camp counselor.

The rest join in, hunched forward, drumming the floor.

Who are these crazy, crazy, unbalanced nutzoids? I came here today totally believing the Donner robotics team wouldn't stalk The Ruler. Now? I'm not so sure. Let me outta here before I get sucked into their twilight zone.

I glance at the clock on the wall. I just donated almost an hour of my life to the Donner Dementos.

I'm coming, Josh!

chapter
seven

I'm up and outta the frightening robotics meeting faster than you can say "Josh Morton."

As I storm through the door, Claire's bossy voice charges after me. "Be at the practice competition at Emerson Middle School's gym. Monday evening."

"Six o'clock," Austin echoes after her.

I'm blazing a path to the pool, sparks practically flashing off my ballet slippers.

Please let me find the pool quickly. Please don't let the game be over.

I hear a whistle blast.

I hear applause and yells.

I burst through the entrance to the pool and skid onto the deck. I scan the water. Eric swims over to

Josh, and they high-five. The ref shows two fingers to the students keeping score in the booth. Two. Josh's number. Which means Josh just scored. I look at the scoreboard. Five to four. For us.

"You rock, Josh!" a girl shrieks. "You so rock, Josh!"

It's Candy. Her arms fluttering above her head and her too-short skirt flapping above her thighs, she's dancing in the bleachers.

The ref blows one long whistle. Game over.

Ack. Eek. Ike. I missed the game. Which Candy saw. I missed Josh's winning goal. Which Candy saw.

The players climb out of the water and walk in a line, shaking hands with the opposing team. When Josh passes me, I clap loudly. He doesn't turn to look at me. No way he can hear me over Candy, who's still screaming his name. Yuck. He waves at her. Double yuck.

I stroll over to the bleachers, bottom level, right side. Basically, as far away as possible from screeching Candy. I sit. Elbows balanced on my knees, I hold my chin and wait. Josh is not going to be happy with me. I watch some of the next game, without really seeing it. Don't even ask me what teams are playing; I couldn't tell you.

Candy sashays by. She shakes her head and her sad limp ponytail at me, saying, "Did you even catch one minute of the game?"

One minute? I'm lucky if I caught one part of one second. I stand. Then I push past Candy, brushing shoulders with her, and head toward the boys' locker room. The water polo players are exiting, done with their team meeting, done with their showers. Josh saunters out, his hair still wet, combed flat and cute. He bounds straight to me. Yeah, I did miss his game. And yeah, Candy did scream her guts out for him. But who's he taking to a sit-down restaurant to celebrate their two-month anniversary? Me, me, me. So there, Candy Lopez!

Josh reaches for my hand and we walk, legs in sync, to the parking lot. Dumb as it sounds, it's only now that I think, Yikeserama, I better not run into someone from the robotics club. I look around wildly, swiveling my head.

"What are you doing?" Josh asks.

"Just admiring the campus."

"Sherry, you crack me up." Josh breaks into a jog, pulling me along with him. "I see my mom's car."

Works for me. I wanna hightail it out of Donner. We slide into his mom's Ford, me in the front passenger seat and him in the back. Josh's mom is a hairdresser named Vicki. With gorgeous highlights, cool shoes and awesome long, fake nails. Vicki gives new meaning to the word "gabby." I think the radio station must be on all day in the beauty salon because she's always up on the news. And she always has opinions. Like today, she yaks for the entire ride about the paparazzi taking pictures of movie stars and their babies. No one tells me which restaurant we're going to, and I don't ask. I figure it's all part of Josh's plan, to make it a surprise.

Vicki pulls up in front of a Mexican restaurant.

Tio Roberto's.

My chest goes tight.

I stare at the green and white neon sign with its dancing sombrero in the corner. I so know this restaurant, from the basket of warm tortilla chips you get before the meal to the striped cinnamon candies you get after. My family used to come here on a regular basis. There are a ton of other Mexican restaurants nearer to my house, but we'd make the drive because of my mother's crazy cravings for their chicken chimichangas. I haven't been back to Tio Roberto's since she died.

"I know how into Mexican you are, Sherry," Josh says, all proud of his choice. "And I heard this place has great food."

Swallowing hard, I turn in my seat and give him a thumbs-up.

He pushes down on the door handle. "Let's kick it in Tio Roberto's."

"Sorry again I couldn't make your game, Josh. Too many heads to cut and color and style. I'll be back to get you two in about an hour when I'm between clients," Vicki says. "And, Sherry, I like your hair. It's fuller than usual."

"Thanks." Maybe I don't look so bad with my portal-of-pain do.

Josh and I open our doors at the exact same moment. We're going to have a rocking sixty-minute date. Despite the tightness in my chest.

Vicki rolls down her window. "Josh, you remember how to calculate the tip?"

"We'll be fine, Mom."

Josh and I spring up the tile steps, past the fountain with an embarrassing sculpture of a half-naked woman pouring water from a bucket on her shoulder, then through the front door. A waitress leads us across the room to a corner table. We get settled in with a basket of chips, a bowl of green salsa, a bowl of red salsa and a dish of spicy carrots.

She brings us water and menus. "I'll give you a few minutes to look this over."

The lighting's kind of low, but not so low that you can't see your meal. Or the chlorine highlights in the shaggy hair of the adorable boyfriend sitting across the table. Or his Lake Havasu blue eyes smiling at you. On the other side of the room, a man in a gray and red poncho plays the guitar and sings in Spanish. We look over the menu and decide what to get. We are so grown-up.

"Did you catch much of my game?" Josh asks.

I dip a chip in green salsa. "Not too much."

"How come?"

"The Ruler." Which isn't entirely false.

"At least you saw me nail that sweet final goal."

I never have to answer because the waitress shows up and takes our order.

"Man. I hope that wasn't my last game." His voice is all sad, not the voice of a guy who just snagged the winning goal.

"What are you talking about? Your last game?" I dip another chip. "The season's not over."

"My grades." Josh shakes his head. "I might end up ineligible."

"No way." I plunk down my glass in surprise. "Your grades are that bad?"

He grimaces. "I didn't realize how bad they were until Coach talked to me in the locker room."

"So, doing the English project with Candy could really help?"

"Yeah. Well, that and one other class, well, two other classes need to fall into place." Josh doesn't meet my eyes as he grabs a carrot.

I reach across the table and touch his arm. "It'll work out, Josh."

The waitress arrives with our food. "Be careful. The plates are hot."

After she sets my meal down, I lean over the steaming food, close my eyes and inhale. The Baja Burrito. My fave burrito in the universe: refried beans + potatoes + spicy beef + guac + cheese. The smell takes me back a couple of years. To the last time I was here with my mom, dad and Sam for my brother's birthday.

The guitar guy hung out by our table and played a bunch of pretty bad music. Until my mom paid him to move along. I gave Sam some great gag gifts like a squirt gun calculator and a whoopee cushion. Dad tied birthday balloons to Sam's ears right before Sam knocked over his Dr Pepper. We had a sweet time. Really sweet.

I pick up the burrito and nibble. Then another nibble. It's okay. But just okay. It's not the burrito of my past.

Maybe Tio Roberto's changed chefs. Or recipes. Or maybe I need Sam next to me, kicking me under the table. Or my mom taking forever to eat her chimichanga. Or my dad making his same-o lame-o "cold today, hot tamale" joke.

A lump like a Ping-Pong ball forms in my throat. I swallow past it. The burrito hasn't changed. My life has.

Josh takes a humongous bite. "Awesome, babe. Even better than any burrito I ate in San Diego." That's where Josh is originally from. And that's saying a lot for this burrito because Josh is way keen on California Mexican food.

I sip my water, willing my throat lump to shrivel up and disappear.

"You know anything about The Ruler's after-school tutoring?" Josh asks.

"It's good. I had to go."

"I'm gonna try it." He spoons extra salsa into his burrito. "You know, to raise my math grade." He takes another big bite. He likes to eat a lot, especially after a game.

With my fork, I push Spanish rice around while Josh wolfs down his food.

"Aren't you hungry?" Josh asks.

"Not as much as you. I didn't just play an amazing water polo game." I scoot my plate toward him. "Plus, I'm saving room for fried ice cream."

"Thanks, Sherry." Josh spears a chunk of avocado. "Guess what? I'm gonna be making some money. My dad's worker quit. I'm gonna get to dig trenches for the sprinkler system at this new apartment complex." Josh pops the avocado into his mouth. "I'll take you on another date."

How romantic. He wants to spend his first paycheck on me. But next time I'm suggesting an unsad place like KFC. "How will you fit in tutoring and water polo and digging?" And me?

He picks up my burrito. "It'll be busy. Like tomorrow I have polo practice, English project with Candy and one section of the apartment's front lawn to dig."

Yikes. Josh is going to be crazy busy, and I'll be tied up with the stalker mystery—hanging with The Ruler, meeting with my mom and Junie, going to Donner robotics meetings, investigating clues. Eek. Candy'll see more of Josh than I will.

The waitress brings our fried ice cream. Josh digs in. One look at my family's fave dessert, and it's like two Ping-Pong balls are lodged in my throat. It's a miracle I can even breathe and haven't keeled over in a dead faint on Tio Roberto's could-be-cleaner floor.

After the waitress drops off the bill, Josh picks it up and stares at the numbers, a cute pencil-thin wrinkle across his adorable forehead. Finally, he un-Velcroes his wallet, pulls out a couple of dollars for the tip and flattens them next to his plate.

At the front of the restaurant, Josh pays the bill. I snag a few cinnamon candies from a ceramic bowl by the cash register. For Sam.

It's dusk outside. His mom's not here yet, so we plop down on the curb.

"Thanks for dinner," I say, knocking my knee against his. "It was really cool of you to plan something for our anniversary."

Josh is beaming. "You're welcome, Sherry. I had a good time." He puts his arm around me. "I always have a good time with you."

I suddenly remember something I keep forgetting to say to him. "Thank you so much for the gorgeous flowers this morning."

Josh's beautiful snapdragon blue eyes open wide. "What flowers?"

chapter
eight

It's Saturday, about two in the afternoon. Junie's over. We did our homework and now we're cross-legged on my bed, painting our nails with this really fun photochromic polish. Mine changes from blue to green in the sun. Hers changes from lilac to rose. She's definitely more interested in clothes and makeup lately. Finally, my best friend is growing up.

"Junie, keep your hand flat. I'll get the polish on more evenly." I make a broad brushstroke down the middle of her nail.

"If Josh didn't send you the flowers, who did?" She glances at the vase on my dresser.

I shrug. "At first, I was thinking maybe I have a secret admirer."

"Yeah, right."

I ignore her sarcasm. "Anyway, the card did say 'Happy Anniversary.' So the secret-admirer theory doesn't fit."

"Maybe the flowers were delivered to the wrong house." Junie blows on her nails. "Maybe one of your neighbors had an anniversary, and the flowers were delivered to your address by mistake."

I shake my head. "There was a Post-it with our address stuck to the cellophane around the bouquet."

"Maybe the flowers were meant for The Ruler. And your dad arranged for the delivery while he's out of town."

"It's not their anniversary. You know they just got married over spring break."

"Could be an anniversary for something else."

There's silence while we both consider this. Then, at the exact same second, we both squeal, "Ewww."

My face all scrunched up, I say, "So I might've taken the flowers my dad sent to The Ruler for their first date or first kiss or something? And she doesn't even know she got flowers? She still thinks they're for me? Grooooss."

"It's a distinct possibility. Why don't you ask your dad?"

"Believe me, I will. I talk to him every day. It's almost like he's not out of town, we hear from him so much."

Junie waves her hand in the air, letting my perfect

polish job dry. "Got any nail jewels? I feel like going all out."

"Wow." I slap her shoulder. "What's with you?"

Her face reddens. Which happens easily because she's hugely freckled.

Anyway, I better stop teasing her. I've been trying forever to get Junie more interested in makeup and clothes and how she looks. You know, to catch up with me socially. And if I tease her too much, she might regress.

From my nightstand, I pull out an envelope loaded with nail jewels and decals.

"Do you think my lips are on the thinnish side?" I jut my face toward Junie's.

She looks surprised. "Say what?"

While I'm telling her about Candy, I get off the bed and root around in my desk for a ruler. "Let's measure our lips."

Junie sighs, but untangles her legs and follows me into the bathroom.

I get up close and personal with the mirror above the sink. I press the ruler against my top lip, then my bottom lip. "One-quarter inch and one-half inch. I'm guessing that's below average width."

Junie takes the ruler and measures hers. She gasps. "One-eighth inch and three-eighths inch. If your lips are too thin, what does that say about mine? And you've already got better eyebrows."

The eyebrow thing is true, so I don't comment. "Wear lip liner and draw your lips bigger," I suggest.

"That's my plan."

Junie sighs. "Once you start with makeup, it never ends."

Also true, so I don't comment again.

We trundle back to my room, where Junie chooses a few nail decorations. She ignores the butterflies and flowers and goes straight for the geometric shapes.

I glue a black spiral onto her index finger. "About the stalker . . ."

"What do we really know about The Ruler? Why would anyone want to stalk her?" Junie sounds so TV cop show. "We know she taught middle school somewhere else, probably in Phoenix, before coming to our school last year. We know she's married to your dad. We know she's obsessed with robotics." With her free hand, she counts off the points. "That's not much. I say we Google her."

"I like your thinking!" I finish off her nails and we head downstairs to our midget office. The Ruler took Sam to Little League practice, and then they're going shopping for new cleats. Phew. That would've been way odd—Googling her while she was in another room.

I boot up the Dell, tap in Google's address and type in "Paula Paulson."

There's an entry for The Ruler with our school website and the robotics club.

Right under it is an entry for a Polly Paulson.

Which I click on.

Polly Paulson.

A psychic.

"She's done readings for lots of different people," Junie says, skimming the screen.

"I wonder how many bad readings she's done," I say. "You know, where she told people stuff they didn't want to hear. Like you're going to have a horrible life or you'll never get the guy you love."

Junie clicks all over the site. "There's no photo of her. I'm curious to see if she looks anything like The Ruler."

Like it's the Fourth of July in my mind, I'm sparking on the bad readings idea. "What if she went into a trance and said stuff to the police like, 'I see this guy in my mind. There he is breaking into the bank. Yup. He's drilling into the safe. And now I see him hiding the money.'"

Another spark flashes in my brain. "Then the police catch the guy and lock him up. And he has a cell mate with a lot of insider info who tells him, 'You were nailed by a psychic named Polly Paulson.'" *Spark.* "So now he's out of prison and stalking The Ruler." *Spark.* "Why? Because he's mixed up. He thinks she's the psychic who fingered him." *Spark.* "And maybe he has big big plans for revenge."

"Sherry, slow down."

But there's no slowing me down. "Maybe our bad guy has bad hearing. From too many prison fights where he got smacked in the ears." *Spark.* "Which means instead of 'Polly Paulson,' he hears 'Paula Paulson.'" I am so on a roll. "The Ruler could be the victim of mistaken-identity stalking!"

"I don't know, Sherry." Junie frowns. "It seems pretty out-there."

Sometimes, in detective work, you have to take giant leaps. Definitely difficult for Junie, who is logical and practical and lives life step-by-step. Not me, though. I'm a leaper. Practically part kangaroo.

I click on "Events with Polly." "Junie, she's at a psychic fair. In Chandler. Today."

"We can go check it out." She's not leaping, but at least she's hopping.

"Can your mom or dad drive us? The Ruler won't be back for hours."

"They're working today."

Junie's parents are both workaholic engineers. Junie's family is just her and her parents, and all three of them are major brainiacs.

"Call Amber," I say. "She can drive us."

Junie stops nodding.

Amber is Junie's gorgeous, blond, stylish, boy-expert, seventeen-year-old cousin. She's a senior in high school, works part-time at the makeup counter of the department store at the mall and is never without at least one boyfriend. Amber's not always nice to us, but she does have her driver's license and a car.

"Come on," I wheedle. "You know you want to see what Polly Paulson looks like. I'm thinking accent, turban, crystal ball, wrinkled, with hairs growing from a mole on her chin."

Her tongue between her teeth, Junie's deciding on a description. "I'll say thin, big earrings, lots of shiny bracelets."

"Loser buys winner a Slurpee." I fake sucking from a straw.

Junie flips open her cell and scrolls through her address book. "I'll text her."

I lean over Junie's shoulder, watching the phone screen.

```
Junie:  wut r ya doing?
Amber:  workin. 10 min to go. Y?
Junie:  There's a psychic u should
go c.
Amber:  Y?
Junie:  2 find out abt ur love
life.
```

66

Amber: Y?

Junie: cuz u just switched boyfriends.

Amber: dat true

Junie: Sherry & I want 2 go 2.

Amber: Y?

Junie: we have ?s.

Amber: so?

Junie: we told you abt the psy-chic, so u should take us 2.

Amber: Y?

Junie: we'll give you gas $.

Amber: ok. Pick u up in 20.

chapter
nine

Junie, me, Amber and Amber's überskinny friend, Dana, are in downtown Chandler, standing on a sidewalk and waiting in line to get into a park. It's a large flat, grassy area, bordered by a low Western-style wooden fence.

"The psychic fair's here?" Amber doesn't actually say, "Pathetic excuse for a psychic fair that's set up outside instead of in a swanky, mirrored, air-conditioned building," but you can hear it in her voice.

Junie and I nod, then shuffle forward. Sometimes—make that, usually—it's better not to call Amber on her attitude. The two older girls follow us.

Sitting in a plastic chair behind a card table, a

woman with a rainbow turban and a matching shawl collects money.

"Love your turban," I say. A blue raspberry Slurpee is clearly in my future.

"Five dollars for entry into the fair," she says. "Readings are ten dollars, payable to the psychic."

After we pay, Turban Lady stamps the back of our hand with the date.

I was expecting a more mystical stamp, like a star or moon or crystal ball. Now I just feel like I'm at the school library.

"There's food in the tent at the far corner of the park." Turban Lady points over her shoulder with the stamp. "The exhibits are throughout the grounds."

"Let's check out the exhibits first," I say.

Tables are set up helter-skelter. The gazillion different colors from various tablecloths and posters and flyers make me feel like I'm trapped in a kaleidoscope. Incense burns on several of the tables, so there's this strange mixture of smells. It's noisy, like at the start of class before the teacher walks in.

"Amber, we so have to see a psychic," Dana says. "I just don't know who to go to the spring dance with." Dana has poufy brown hair. Which she flips back with a jerky hand movement, like she's under a blinking strobe light.

"Who asked you?" Amber says.

69

"Ryan and Jesse." Dana flips her hair. Flips it again.

"You don't need a psychic for that." Amber's looking past Dana, scanning the area. "Go with Ryan. Obviously."

"Ryan?" *Flip.* "Why?" *Flip.*

Amber's finished surveying. Her eyes back on Dana, she shoots her the do-I-really-have-to-explain-this look. Like Dana asked something way simple à la should you buy your jeans a size too small or so they fit? Holding up a finger topped with a long violet nail for each point in his favor, Amber says, "Ryan has a car. Ryan has cuter hair. Ryan has a cool part-time job at Electronics City. Ryan has an older brother with lots of friends."

Arms hanging limp by her side, Dana says, "Well, I still want psychic advice about my dress."

Amber and Dana ditch us. I'm sure we cramp their style. Not that you really need style here; it's mostly old women wearing flowing, baggy dresses and dangly earrings.

Junie and I wander from table to table. We're eyeballing name tags and pamphlets, on the lookout for Polly Paulson. She's going to be tougher to find than I thought, because there are lots of people milling about and lots of booths. Luckily, we're not in a huge rush. The Ruler's not picking us up for a couple of hours. Amber and Dana are leaving earlier to hit an R-rated movie.

We come to a table with really cute figurines and jewelry and polished stones. I'm fingering an adorable amethyst necklace.

A guy with long hair and tattoos up and down his arms says, "That stone offers very powerful protection against the spirit world."

I must have a blank look on my face because he continues, "If you spend any time at all contacting spirits, amethysts are necessary for your safety."

Really? Sounds like a must-have item for me.

"Actually, we're trying to find Polly Paulson," Junie says.

"Yeah, Polly's here. She's cool. You friends of hers?"

I give my mysterious, could-be-yes-could-be-no smile. "Where's she at?"

He waves toward the back of the park and turns to help another customer. We walk in that general direction, passing tables that offer readings by tarot cards or tea leaves or palms. And tables with gypsyish clothing. And a table where you can have your blood analyzed. And a table manned by someone with a long papier-mâché wand with special healing powers.

Tucked away in the far corner, an Avon lady has a sign advertising free perfume samples with a tarot card reading. She doesn't have any customers and is skimming a magazine while sipping on a Starbucks.

Junie points at the Avon lady. "Sherry, let's do it."

I'm shocked. I'm dismayed. I grasp the nearest

table so that I don't fall over in a dead faint. "Junie, you don't even wear perfume."

"Hey, I might start."

As my grandma Baldwin would say, something strange is going on in the universe. "Maybe she's Polly Paulson."

Walking all purposeful, Junie approaches the Avon lady. "Excuse me. Are you Polly Paulson?"

She looks up from her magazine and laughs. "Polly? You've obviously never met her."

This statement makes me nervous, like maybe Polly Paulson has vampire fangs or two heads or is half woman, half cyclops.

"She went for a bite to eat." The Avon lady closes her magazine and picks up her cards.

"Here?" I say. "Is Polly eating here?"

The Avon lady fingers the tips of the cards. "Yes, in the food tent." She looks up at us, especially at Junie. "You want a reading?"

"Come on, Junie," I say, already taking a step away.

"Maybe later," Junie says.

I'm off like a shot.

Junie's behind me, wheezing like the out-of-shape girl she is.

I dash past a whiteboard easel with the menu written on it and through the opening into the food tent. Which is deceptively larger than it looks from the outside. There are only a few people here. Not surprising, given the food they're serving: carrot juice, falafel, organic salad. Without even waiting for Junie, I march straight to the counter and say, breathlessly, to the wrinkled woman stacking tan napkins, "Do you know if Polly Paulson is here?"

Index finger holding the napkins in place, she surveys the room. "That's her in the corner." She points with her free hand and calls out, "Polly, some people here to see you."

My eyes follow the direction she's indicating, and I gasp.

I can totally see why Tattoo Guy thought Polly and me might be friends.

Polly is, like, our age.

She has long, überthick blond hair with sky blue streaks. She blinks; her eyelids are coated in the same blue. She looks like she's my petite size of five feet two and exactly one hundred pounds.

Junie finally catches up and pants by my side.

Polly Paulson pokes the last bite of her falafel into her mouth and gives a friendly wave.

"That's her," I say.

Junie's jaw drops.

"No Slurpees for us," I say.

We pick our way through the tables to where Polly's sitting. Polly pulls down on the back of her Pretty Punk T-shirt. "You guys want a reading?" She has a great smile.

"I do," Junie says quickly, like she's volunteering for extra credit at school.

Polly stands, swings a black backpack over her shoulder. "I'm done with my break. Let's go back to my area."

"You're really Polly Paulson?" I ask, walking next to her.

"Yup."

"And you're psychic?"

"Yeah. It basically runs in my family."

"And you're how old?"

"Thirteen. You?"

"Same." A thirteen-year-old psychic with a punk-rock T-shirt and blue hair streaks? Sounds sketchy to me. "Have you ever done any psychic work for the police?"

"No. Why?"

"Just curious."

Polly gives me a funny look.

I may be forced to rethink the whole The-Ruler-is-a-victim-of-mistaken-identity-stalking theory.

"Can I go first?" Junie asks.

What has come over scientifically minded Junie?

"Works for me." Polly flashes her great smile again. We pass the Avon lady.

"Hi, Mom," Polly says to her. "I'll watch your table if you want to go to lunch now."

Junie, Miss Never-Fazed-by-a-Pop-Quiz, gapes open-mouthed for the second time in five minutes. My jaw's on the ground too.

Polly points to a folding metal chair. "Have a seat," she says to Junie.

Junie pulls a ten-dollar bill from her purse.

"Thanks," Polly says. Then she drags a matching chair from behind the table and plunks herself down so that they're sitting across from each other, their knees practically touching. Polly looks at Junie, totally making eye contact.

Junie breaks the gaze and glances at me. "Do you mind if this is private?"

Is the earth suddenly flat? Will there be two moons in the sky tonight? Will I start speaking French in my sleep? Junie, my best friend, actually wants to have a *secret* psychic reading. Without me.

"Uh, okay," I say.

I wander over to an exhibit of clothing and purses. I pick up a clutch and play with the clasp. *Open, close. Open, close.* I'm not really noticing anything, still kind of flabbergasted at Junie's behavior. I keep an eye on the two of them, their heads close together. After about five minutes, they sit straight, like they're wrapping things up. I walk back and stand behind Junie.

"Definitely watch for some developments in your love life. Real soon," Polly says.

Developments in Junie's love life? What love life?

Junie's not even into boys. Which she'll happily tell you. She doesn't have time, what with keeping up her perfect grades and applying to astronaut summer camp and being prez of the Latin club. I, on the other hand, am so into boys. Due to the fact that I'm socially advanced. Developments in Junie's love life? Ha! Unless Junie does have her eye on Eric, Polly's a big, bogus fake.

Junie beams at Polly. "Thank you," she says.

That's one of the things I love about my best friend; she's genuinely nice. With all the love-life mumbo jumbo, Junie must know Polly's a phony-baloney, but she still thanks her.

When Junie vacates the chair, I slide in and say, "You can stay." I smile sweetly.

"Oh, okay." Junie hangs beside me.

I hold out my money to Polly, who tucks it away in a pink pencil box, then takes my hands.

There's an instant connection. Not like electrical tingling or anything like that. More like we're pulling on Silly Putty, stretching it out so we're joined in a loose, rubbery way.

Polly's silent, just staring at me, making a connection with our eyes too. Then she's gazing off across the room.

"It's all shimmery," Polly says.

I'm tapping my foot. All shimmery? What kind of lame psychic gibberish is that?

"Oh, I see." Polly squinches up her eyes. "It's a pool. A swimming pool."

I tap a little slower.

"It's a guy with kind of messy hair. He's talking to a girl." She pauses. "Not you."

I quit tapping altogether.

"The girl's talking, talking, talking to him. I can't hear any words, though. Standing too close to him. Glitter everywhere. You know what? He's not interested in her." Polly pins me with her eyes. "He likes you. A lot."

Is she seeing Josh and Candy? No, no, no. I set my foot to tapping again. Because in Phoenix, everyone has a pool. Because every girl I know, except Junie, is crushing on a guy. Because it's nothing for two girls to want the same dude. Because we all love glitter.

"More water." Polly's grip tightens on my hands. "Not a pool, though." She's silent for a second. "It's an aquarium. You have fish?"

"Yeah. Bala sharks." My foot hangs midair, uncertain as to whether it should tap or not.

"Are they sick? Or maybe they're gonna get sick. Something. You need to take good care of them."

You can bet your booty on that; I am no negligent fish owner.

With a head jerk, Polly's staring off. Way off. Like at a park two states over. "I see a woman." She's talking in a low, sleepy voice with lots of pauses. It's like she's choosing her words super carefully, the way you choose your eye shadow to match your outfit. "Slender . . . stands very straight . . . beige outfit." She stops.

My heart stops too. My arms go all chilly and goose bumpy. It's The Ruler!

Polly blinks chameleon-slow, showing lots of blue eyelid. "She's outside. . . . There's a knife . . . a sharp knife . . . glinting in the sun."

My foot may never tap again.

Polly shakes her head, like she's trying to get rid of a scary thought. "Whoever this woman is, she needs to seriously watch out." Polly drops my hands.

And my arms immediately stiffen up and lose their wobbliness.

Polly's eyes focus. "Who is she?"

"The Ruler," Junie whispers. "Sherry's stepmom."

And at that very second, my cell phone rings. Well, more like makes waterfall + loon sounds.

It's The Ruler.

chapter
ten

"Hello," I squeak. I clear my throat. "Hello."

"Sherry!" The Ruler says fast and high. "Is Amber still there?"

"Amber?" I'm confused.

"See if she can bring you and Junie home."

"See if Amber can bring me and Junie home?" I repeat like a just-woke-up, clueless person.

"Why?" Junie says to me.

"Why?" I parrot into the phone.

"It's my car." Now The Ruler's voice is shaky. "The tires, Sherry. Someone slashed my tires."

"Someone slashed your tires?" I'm squeaking again.

Junie's eyes are round as hubcaps.

Polly's eyes are fixed on me.

"With a knife?" I say. "Did they slash them with a knife?"

"That would be my guess." The Ruler takes a rattly breath. "Right now I'm waiting at home for the police to show up."

Junie's on her cell, texting Amber. She gives me a thumbs-up.

"It works for Amber," I tell The Ruler.

"Good, good," she says.

"Why don't you have a cup of that chamomile tea stuff. That's the calming one, right?" I say. "And call Dad."

Of course, now is the time my dad picks to be out of town. Right when freaky-deaky things are happening. Like stalkers going after The Ruler. Like psychic readings coming true. Like car tires getting slashed.

I slowly press the End button. "Polly, who slashed the tires?"

"I don't know. I'm sorry." She really does look sorry. "I told you exactly what I was seeing. You know everything I know."

Junie pokes me in the side. "We better meet up with Amber."

Suddenly, I feel in a hurry to get home. I wanna check out the tire situation and The Ruler. "Where *is* Amber?" I stand and push in my chair.

Her eyebrows up in a question, Junie looks at Polly. "At a ghost hunter's booth. Where's that?"

"The other side of the park. In a tent. Kitty-corner to here." Polly stands. She hands me her business card. "Sherry, you need to be careful."

"Whaddya mean?"

"I didn't see anything specific. Just this general dark cloud of danger around you." Polly moves her chair. "You're not psychic. But you've got something, Sherry. You know it, right?"

I shrug. "Yeah."

"Call me if you need me." Polly touches my shoulder.

"Come on." Junie grabs my hand and we take off through the exhibits, dodging people and tables. We jog past the food tent to one with a handwritten sign: THE GHOST HUNTER.

Inside the tent, Amber, Dana and a guy are huddled over a table. Their backs are to us.

The guy says, "It's a gaussmeter. Brand-new and very expensive. I use it to determine paranormal presences when I'm on a ghost call."

"Amber," Junie calls.

The three of them straighten and turn around.

Can you say "Cutie-Pie Ghost Hunter"? No wonder Amber's hanging out here. Mr. Ghost Hunter's the most adorable older guy in history. He's, like, twenty and very Hollywood, with blond-brown hair and piercing dark eyes. Granted, the whole ghost-hunter persona is bizarro, but you kind of forget about that when you're looking at him.

He glides over to us. "I'm Zane."

He shakes our hands. Too odd. I mean, we're thirteen. Usually twenty-year-olds ignore us. "What can I do for you two?" His voice is like fondue chocolate.

"Uh, nothing." Junie looks around him to Amber. His cuteness is not sidetracking her. "Amber, let's go. You gotta take us to Sherry's house."

Smoothing out her T-shirt, Amber steps toward Zane. "What's the rush? The tires are already wrecked."

Junie shakes her head with impatience. "The rush is you need to drive us back to Sherry's before you and Dana go to the movies."

"Movies?" Amber says, ogling Zane like she doesn't have a boyfriend. Which she does, but she likes to have more than one. That way she always has a guy to hang out with that she's not tired of. Of course, if she had a high-caliber boyfriend like Josh, she wouldn't be going for quantity over quality.

Junie's freckles are 3-D, standing out like they always do when she gets frustrated. "The movie you and Dana are going to. You know, the reason you couldn't give us a ride home in the first place."

"Oh, that movie." Amber sidles up close to Zane. "We're not going anymore. Instead, we're learning all about the ghost-hunting business. Right, Dana?"

"I guess." Dana isn't smiling.

"I'd really like to get home. I'm kinda worried about The Ruler." I pull my phone from my pocket and glance at the time. "How about five more minutes here, then we head out?"

Zane springs with enthusiasm back to the table of equipment. He carefully picks up a yellow rectangular box with a plastic handle on top. A rubber hose with a metal end snakes out from the back. Totally reminds me of my old Fisher-Price cassette player + microphone.

"This is a Geiger counter. It scientifically measures electromagnetic radiation," Zane says. "So I can tell if there's ghost activity in a particular setting." He holds it like it's real gold. "I made it myself."

Amber's hanging on his every word. Dana looks less convinced.

Junie's up close at the table, examining the equipment. "This is the gaussmeter?" She points to a black box about the size of a calculator, but thicker.

Zane carefully lays down the Geiger counter, coiling the hose around its base. He lovingly picks up the gaussmeter. "It is."

"Is it the same thing as a magnetometer?"

Zane's eyes open wide in surprise. He's not used to dealing with people like Junie who're chock-full of engineering genes. "It is."

"Can I see what it looks like on?"

"Sure. It's charged." He prods the switch to On and the skinny needle on the screen wiggles like a hula dancer, then settles in at zero.

Ack. Eek. Ike. I smell coffee. It's my mother. Apparently she found the note I left her about the psychic fair. I stuck it under a pile of espresso beans in our usual meeting place, the pear tree in our backyard.

The gaussmeter needle starts hopping.

"I don't believe it!" Zane says. "We're showing activity." He starts striding around the room, the meter cradled in his palm.

On the table, a couple of metal rods clang against each other.

"Grab the Geiger counter!" Zane says to Junie, his voice quivering with excitement.

She picks it up and turns it on. The rubber hose bounces in the air. She grabs it.

"What can I do? What can I do?" Amber's pogoing up and down, minus the pogo stick.

"Camera!" Zane's gone bug-eyed. "I haven't seen activity this strong in a while. Watch for ectoplasmic mist, Amber." He's walking toward me.

"Hi, Sherry," Mom says. "What's going on?"

I whiz to the corner of the tent, figuring she'll follow me. I turn my back on everyone. "The equipment's sensing you, Mom. You gotta get outta here."

"Dana," Zane says, "close the flap. Beginner ghosts have trouble with thresholds. Let's see if we can trap this one in here."

"What makes you think this is a beginner ghost?" I call over my shoulder, doing my best to not sound defensive.

"Coming here, with all this equipment." Zane doesn't even look up from the meter. "A seasoned ghost would know better."

"I can't get out." Mom's panicking.

"Junie." I wave her over to me.

As she gets closer, the Geiger counter clickety-clicks like it's having seizures. Junie's fighting with the hose, which surges and sways around her face.

"It's my mom!" I whisper.

She goes still. All it takes is a millisecond. A millisecond of not paying attention to the excited rubber hose.

Whap. It smacks her ear.

"Ow!" Junie yells. She drops the Geiger counter.

I scoop it up before it hits the floor. I turn it off and set it down.

Then I cover my mouth with my hand and, doubled over, race across the room. "Gonna barf. Gonna barf."

I throw open the tent flap.

Mom whooshes out with a breathy "Catch you later."

I sink down to the grass; my head flops against my knees. I'm sweating buckets.

Finally, Junie comes out and sits next to me. "You okay, Sherry?"

"That call was too crazy close, Junie. He knew my mom was there. He wanted to trap her. Who knows what he would've done to her. Yikes."

"Your mother needs to stay way far away from Zane and his equipment." Junie rubs my back. "Definitely."

Amber and Dana arrive. "You're not going to throw up in my car, are you?" Amber asks.

That girl has about as much sympathy as a rock. I shake my head. "I'm good now."

Junie stands and pulls me to my feet.

While we're driving, Amber says to Dana, "Sherry is, like, Junie's weirdest friend. You have no idea."

I don't even have the energy to tell her to be quiet.

Amber's plan is to drop me off first, then Junie.

Junie, however, has other ideas.

chapter
eleven

When we get to my place, Junie jumps out with me. Over her shoulder, she shouts to Amber, "Give me a sec to check out the tires!"

Junie and I buzz to where The Ruler's hybrid is hanging by the curb. All four tires look the same: sad and saggy with a big cut in a semicircle by the rim. Yikes.

Junie pokes at one of the splits. "Sure looks like you'd need a sharp knife to do this."

"Polly predicted something with a knife *and* outside *and* The Ruler," I say with a shudder.

"Seriously creepy." Junie rubs her arms.

Amber honks.

"I wish I could stay longer," Junie says. "But you

know Amber. Plus, my mom is actually home for dinner."

She takes off and I head inside.

At the kitchen table, The Ruler's frantically sipping a mug of calming chamomile tea. There's a mini mountain of used tea bags on a saucer by the kettle.

Sip, sip, sip. "The police were already here to take photos of the tires. They said it could've been some teens having fun, or maybe it was the work of a disgruntled student. They were surprised that it happened in broad daylight and that none of the neighbors saw anything."

Sip, sip, sip. "I've talked to the insurance company. A tow truck is coming in ten minutes. I'll ride with them to Tires Tires Tires."

Sip, sip, sip. "Grandma Baldwin has Sam."

My ears prick up. Because if Grandma is back from Sedona, then Grandpa, who followed her there, is back too. And he'll help with the mystery.

A few years ago, Grandpa died of a heart attack. He took on the shape of our state bird, a wren, and joined the Academy. His croaky voice is tough to understand, but he's got a great sense of direction and good ideas too.

Grandma, Queen of Birkenstocks, Chants and Aura Combing, hasn't figured out Grandpa's true identity. She thinks he's just a hungry wren who hangs around her bird feeders. Which, by the way, she has about fifty of in her backyard. I'm sure Sam went over to her house to help fill the feeders after Grandma's weekend away. Stocking those feeders is a job and a half. I avoid it.

Sip, sip, sip. "Grandma and Sam will pick me up at the tire place and drive back here. I'll use your father's car until my car's ready."

Polly's warning about The Ruler echoes in my brain: *She needs to seriously watch out.* "Yeah, well, be careful," I say. "Maybe I should come with you."

She stops mid-sip, peering at me over the rim of her mug. "Sherry, I'm fine. Someone ruined my tires. They're not planning to do something to me. I don't want you to worry." *Sip, sip, sip.* "Besides, the towing company will only allow one passenger."

She's so Energizer Bunny. My head's spinning with the complicatedness of all this. So upstairs I trundle for some quiet, thoughtful time with my fish.

In my bedroom, I slide open the aquarium cover. Then I tap in some fish flakes. Cindy and Prince glintily zip to the surface, gobbling floating flakes. I'm careful not to overfeed them. And I'm careful to close the cover, because bala sharks will leap from a tank to their death.

The Ruler calls out to let me know she's leaving. From my window, I watch her climb into the passenger side of the tow truck, and Polly's warning floats into my brain. I do believe The Ruler'll be okay on this short trip to town. But tire slashing? That's scary stuff.

The tow truck clanks away from our curb, The Ruler's car humped on its back. After they're nothing more than a lumpy speck in the distance, I go back to vegging in front of my aquarium.

I'm planning to mull over the mystery, but my brain has other ideas. My thoughts drift to Josh. It's like I'm relaxed and sitting at the edge of the ocean while gentle waves of romance lap at my feet. Polly saw The Ruler stuff, which means she also saw Josh choose me over pushy, glittery Candy.

I'm just hanging there, full of ripply waves of love, in the I-got-the-boy place. My fish, their tummies all full of flakes, are gliding lazily through the water, happy to have each other. I could chill here forever.

My cell rings: "Workin' Overtime" by the Father Figures. It's my dad.

"What is going on out there? Is Paula okay?" he says. "I'm out of town for a couple of weeks, and look what happens."

You'd think my dad would be cooler with wacko situations given that he was married to my mother the cop for so long. But, uh, no.

"I think I better cut this trip short and come home

now," Dad says. "And I'll just come back here next month to finish up."

"Yikes. Stay there and get everything done. So you don't have to go back for a while," I say. "Paula's handling it okay. Although it's definitely gotten to her. But, Dad, remember, either me or Sam are pretty much always here. We'll be a good support."

"And the police believe a student slashed her tires?" he asks, all anxious.

"Dad, chill. They said maybe. Emphasis on the 'may' and the 'be.' Could just be total random violence. As in, Paula's car was in the wrong place at the wrong time."

He makes me promise to keep a watchful eye on The Ruler and Sam and to call him if I see anything strange. Thanks to Verizon, I can actually hear my father's nervous habit from across the miles—he's cracking his knuckles.

"I'm counting on you, Sherry."

"Pinky promise, Dad." I wave my baby finger in the air even though I know he can't see it.

Imagine if he knew the truth. That The Ruler has a stalker. A stalker she doesn't even know about. You have to be übercareful how much you share with parents. Reality often throws them into a tizzy.

Now for some investigating. "Dad, you should send Paula some flowers. You know, to make her feel better." I squeeze my eyes shut, hoping beyond hope that he'll say he just sent a bouquet yesterday, and maybe he should send something else, like a box of fake-o chocolate-carob squares.

"Good thinking, Sherry. I haven't sent her flowers since before the wedding. They'll really perk her up."

Ack!

chapter
twelve

Out to the backyard. My arms up, I jump, then swing a leg over the bottom limb of our ornamental pear tree. The tree my mom planted when I was born. And the place where she first made contact with me. I get all settled, my back rubbing against the rough bark, my legs stretched out and crossed at the ankles. Then I open the plastic bag of espresso beans and wave it back and forth while thinking Mom thoughts. Hopefully, Grandpa will show up too.

"Mom. Mom." I wave the bag. "Anytime now."

Just as I'm about to give up and go grab a Mountain Dew and some Doritos, a breeze rustles the leaves at the top of the tree.

Thud!

I clutch the bag tight to my chest. Mom has got to work on her landing.

"Sorry about that, pumpkin." My branch shakes as Mom settles herself in.

The smell of coffee wraps around me.

"Caw, caw." Grandpa lands by my feet, his ratty wings fluttering furiously, his pink belly pooching out. I guess we're all in a row, me by the trunk, Grandpa sandwiched in the middle, then Mom at the end.

"Yay, Grandpa! You're here."

He flashes me a beaky smile.

The shaking of my branch slows down but doesn't completely stop. Which means Mom is in her fave position, one leg crossed over the other, jiggling a foot.

"Are you okay, Mom?" I ask. "Did the ghost-hunting equipment hurt or anything?"

"No, it didn't hurt," she says.

"You couldn't just lift up the tent flap and leave?" I jam the bag of beans in my pocket.

"I can cross thresholds, but I can't manipulate barriers to get to them," Mom says. "Yet."

"Did you tell Grandpa about the ghost hunter?" I ask.

Grandpa nods, and a feather comes loose and flutters to the ground.

"Did you learn anything of interest at the psychic fair?" Mom asks.

"Uh, yeah. Where's my brain at?" I shift position so the branch isn't digging into my thigh. "The psychic, who's my age, by the way, predicted something bad with The Ruler and a knife. Right after that, The Ruler called because—get this!—someone slashed her tires! All four of them. Flat as pancakes."

"Where's the car?" Mom asks.

"At Tires Tires Tires," I say.

"I'd like to examine the damage," Mom says. "Wilhelm, we'll stop there on the way home." The branch goes still. She must be thinking, twirling her hair around her index finger. "That escalated fast."

"What do you mean?" I ask.

"A stalker's behavior generally escalates or gets worse over time. I'm assuming her stalker is responsible for the tire business," Mom says. "Slashing tires is fairly violent. And risky to undertake during the day. He's not starting off with small actions."

Yikes. I do not want to hear we're dealing with a crazier-than-usual stalker. "The police came, and they're doing a report."

"Good. Although they won't devote much effort to one-time vandalism. *We'll* have to step up our efforts for guarding Paula," Mom says.

Grandpa nods his balding bird head.

"We have to keep her safe," Mom says quietly to him, but I still hear her. "She's what's holding my family together."

Grandpa mutters something about surveillance schedules and the weekend.

"That's right. I'm tied up all this weekend too. Sherry, you'll have to handle surveillance Saturday and Sunday."

"I can," I say. "What's up with you guys?"

Grandpa jabbers. Something so not intelligible to the human ear.

"Uh, Academy business," Mom says.

"Mom, just tell me."

"It's the Annual Worldwide Academy Ghostlympics, where we pit our skills against Academies from various countries, including Germany, France, Spain, Korea. I'm entered in the animal mind-control event." Her voice swells with pride. "It's unusual for a newer student like myself to represent the Academy. But, as you know, I'm good with animals."

She certainly was when she was alive and worked Canine with her springer spaniel, Nero Wolfe. "What do you get as prizes, invisible ribbons?" I crack myself up.

There's silence.

"What? I was joking. There aren't really prizes, are there? I mean, you're adults. And, well, ghosts."

Grandpa jabbers some more in, once again, impossible-to-understand birdspeak.

"There *are* prizes." Mom stops.

Something is going on here. Why won't Mom and Grandpa just spill. "Like what?"

"Sherry, it's a long shot. Grandpa doesn't think we should even aim for it because it's *extremely* difficult to win. So we can't pin our hopes on it," she says, her voice going all bubbly and enthusiastic. "But if I come in first in my division—and that's a big if—I win five minutes of Real Time."

"Real Time?" I say.

"It's exactly what it sounds like." Mom's branch is bouncing up and down like she's jumping with excitement. "Five minutes of regular time with a human. There are minor restrictions, such as the human doesn't remember the time. Although he does carry away the feeling of the time. Sort of an emotional tying up of loose ends. But five whole real minutes!" Her branch bounces again.

Excitement zings through me like I'm those Christmas lights that blink. "Go right this minute and find some animals and bend their thoughts like pretzels." Arm extended, I point my finger out toward the yard. "Go! Go! Go! Five minutes where I could see you and talk with you like normal? Überfantastic!"

Grandpa shakes his balding head.

"First-time Ghostlympians never win," Mom says.

"Stop with the head shaking, Grandpa. Mom can't win if she doesn't try. We have to go for it!"

Grandpa slowly nods.

I stare at where my mother's probably sitting. "Mom! Go directly to the zoo." I'm wagging my finger so hard, it's a blur. "Fly to the zoo! Practice on every single living animal there: bears, rhinos, squirrels, the gross two-headed snake."

Grandpa waves his raggedy wings. "Go, go, go!"

"I will. I'll give it my best shot." She'd probably be high-fiving me if she could. "But"—Mom sucks in a deep breath—"let's finish up here." The branch quits dipping all over the place and goes still. "I went to your school's staff meeting yesterday afternoon. One item of interest. Did you know Paula is failing Kyle Rogers? His dad is president of the school district's board."

"Uh, no. I wouldn't normally know junk like that. All I know is Kyle's an eighth-grade basketball star who, according to Josh, has major attitude."

"Apparently his dad's pretty upset about the F and is leaning hard on your principal, who's leaning hard on Paula to pass him. She won't budge. So there may be something there."

"Junie and I could eat lunch near Kyle and eavesdrop. Could you and Grandpa check out the dad?"

Grandpa's got his beady dark eyes trained right on me. At my questions, he bobs his head.

Mom goes on. "In a nutshell, the staff at Saguaro likes Paula. They even tried the hummus and pita bread she brought to the meeting. And no one, except your principal, wants her to give a freebie passing grade to Kyle."

"Would our principal do anything to The Ruler?" I ask.

"Like stalking? I don't think so. Paula applied for math department head at your school. Perhaps he won't give her a strong recommendation. There's a district meeting on Monday to discuss the candidates. I'll go to that," Mom says. "You know what the staff at Saguaro's really happy about? The robotics club. I gather Paula put Saguaro on the robotics map last year."

"It's true." And I tell them about my Donner robotics-meeting experience. I finish up with, "Those kids are way scary-weird about robotics and they're seriously annoyed with The Ruler. And they have two secret plans, A and B."

Still staring at me, Grandpa says, "Rats blinking, Sherry."

"Yes, fast thinking of you to join their club, Sherry," Mom adds. "Keep a hand in there, and we'll see what you come up with."

"And then there were these mysterious flowers that came with a happy anniversary card," I say. "First I thought they were for me. From Josh. Then I thought they were for The Ruler from Dad. But negative and negative."

"A stalker who sends flowers and slashes tires?" There's a long silence where I just know my mom's doing the hair-twirling thing again. "It doesn't fit any profile I've ever seen. Obviously, there's a mix-up with the flowers," she says, "but I doubt it's related to the stalker. And I don't think we need to pursue it."

Grandpa's small beak opens. "I need to pee."

Which is totally random unless he really said, "I agree."

"How does this sound for our surveillance schedule over the next couple of days?" Mom lists it off. "Anything else before we adjourn?"

"Wait. I wanna know what happened in Sedona," I say. "Did Grandma figure out about Grandpa?"

Ironically, Grandma went all the way to Sedona to take a new age class on how to talk to the spirit world when she's got Grandpa in her own backyard. Poor Grandpa keeps racking his birdy brain to come up with ways to make contact with her. Those two just can't seem to get it together.

Grandpa looks down at the ground. "No contact."

"Sorry." I rub his scraggly elfin head. "I wish I could help you out." But he understands that I can't tell her. Academy rules. Even though Grandma's like the one person who'd believe right off in the ghost stuff.

The branch we're sharing bobs up, like it lost a passenger.

"Sherry, you okay if Grandpa and I go over to the tire place now?"

"And then you're going to practice for the Ghostlympics?"

"Absolutely," Mom says.

"Sure. You guys take off," I slide down from the tree and head to the front yard. It's not that I really think the stalker will come back today, but I promised Dad I'd be vigilant. So, a quick tour around the house, then I'm heading inside to my room, to chill with my fish.

As I round the corner, kicking the odd-shaped gray stones we have instead of a water-sucking lawn, the sun glints off our big ugly bush. Odd. I stop and stare. It happens again. There is nothing silver or glinty or flashy about that bush. Once a year it covers itself with tiny berries. But even then, they're a dull brick red. I walk over to the bush.

I gently pry apart the outer branches. A few shriveled leaves fall to the ground. I peer in.

There, plunged way deep in the heart of the bush, is a knife.

chapter
thirteen

And not just any old knife's stuck in the middle of the ugly bush.

It's a knife I recognize.

The Ginsu kitchen knife Dad ordered from TV for The Ruler. The long, pointy, never-needs-sharpening, $19.95, shipping-and-handling-extra Ginsu knife.

The stalker used one of The Ruler's knives! From our kitchen! The stalker was in our house! Ack. Eek. Ike.

I gulp air for a few minutes, then pull myself together.

I march into the kitchen, straight to the drawer with the Saran Wrap and tinfoil and plastic bags, and grab a pair of disposable gloves. The Ruler uses them when handling raw meat. Basically, with her in the house, we're equipped for every kind of emergency. In this case, we're talking about picking up a piece of evidence without smudging the fingerprints. Thanks to my prior detecting experience, I know all about fingerprints.

Yanking on the gloves, I march back to the big ugly bush. Then I plunge both arms in.

Yikes. The knife's totally stuck in the bush. With some heavy breathing and a hefty pull, I free the knife.

Then I'm stumbling and waving the knife in the air, trying to catch my balance.

Just as The Ruler and Sam and Grandma Baldwin pull into the driveway.

The Ruler leaps out of the passenger side of Grandma's car. "Sherry! Are you okay? What's going on?"

Grandma follows. She stops to pull up her kneesocks and slide her feet into her Birkenstock sandals.

Sam climbs out slowly, his eyes on the knife.

I lower it to my side. "I think this is what the person wrecked the tires with."

The Ruler reaches me. "My Ginsu knife?"

Sam's eyes are growing bigger and bigger, like those spongy figures you leave in water to expand. "The bad guy was in our kitchen." He always makes connections freaky fast. Like he's some kind of midget genius.

"Paula, you should call the police and have them

dust for fingerprints." I'm thinking Mom can sneak into the police station to find out what they come up with. No way we're letting the police crack this case. Mom only gets credit if *we* solve it.

"Fingerprints?" The Ruler looks dazed, which is so not her style. "Oh, so that's why you're wearing plastic gloves."

Grandma shuffles toward me, her arms making big circles in the air, like she's pushing away evil spirits. "Good for you, Sherry, using your noodle."

"I'll call the detective who came out earlier." The Ruler straightens up, totally in her element now that she has a task to fulfill. "His card's inside." She strides to the front door.

No doubt the card is in a special file folder labeled "Tire Incident." The Ruler invented überorganization.

"I'll get started scattering mint leaves by the doors and windows. Keeps intruders out. Snakes too." Grandma clomp-clomps the rest of the way up the walk.

"Sherry, bring that knife inside." Grandma opens the front door. "You and Sam can help me burn some cloves. Then we'll mix the ashes with salt and sprinkle them around the perimeter of the rooms. To keep evil out." She pauses, a finger on her chin. "I'm pretty sure it's good for your love life too."

"She gets more and more nutzoid," I say to Sam, who's sticking to my side.

"Just don't ask her about this wren she thinks she has a"—he makes finger quotes—" 'special relationship' with."

In the kitchen, I gesture to the pantry with my shoulder. "Sam, get me a bag."

He doesn't even question the order, which only proves how creeped out he is.

Grandma grabs a cereal bowl, then pulls open drawers till she finds matches. All pyromaniac, she gets a rinky-dink clove fire going in the bowl.

The Ruler is already on the phone with the detective about the knife and possible fingerprints.

I wrap up the knife nice and safe in a plastic bag and scoot it to the back of the counter. I peel off the disposable gloves and trash them.

Grandma dumps a bunch of salt on top of the clove ashes, then hands me the bowl and a spoon. "Stir it up, would you, Sherry?" She starts another clove fire in a different bowl.

Next she'll be asking me to wear face paint and beat on drums.

The phone pressed against her ear, The Ruler bites her lip, thinking hard. "Actually, my husband may have used the knife last. He was slicing food for the barbecue in the backyard. And now I'm not sure it was ever brought back into the kitchen."

Now that she's said it, I do remember Dad grilling last weekend before he went out of town. He was wearing his dorky chef's apron, the one that says "Old accountants never die, they just lose their balance." I can totally see him humming Céline Dion and slicing pineapple (surprisingly yummy when grilled) and bananas (incredibly gross when grilled).

And then I remember something else. "Sam, I was on cleanup that evening."

"So you probably forgot the knife outside by mistake." Sam's shoulders relax. He's less creeped out if the bad guy wasn't rooting around in our kitchen.

Me too. Although, yikeserama, I basically left out the weapon.

Balancing the phone on her shoulder while she slots the paperwork back in the file, The Ruler frowns. "You won't be out today to get the knife?"

She hangs up and turns to me and Sam. "Well, they'll come by sometime this week for the prints. This case isn't high priority." And then, because she's the master of multitasking and can listen to many conversations at once, like even an entire classroom, she says, "Sherry, if it hadn't been my Ginsu knife, he'd have found something else."

Sam moves closer to me. "I'd probably have left it outside too. If I'd been on cleanup."

Which is totally not true because Sam is Mr. Neat and Tidy.

The Ruler claps. "Kids, I know exactly what'll perk us up. Some of my homemade lentil soup and rosemary bread. First thing tomorrow morning, we'll all make a trip to the Nut 'n' Nut for the ingredients."

Oh yeah, that's definitely what leaps to mind when I'm feeling down. A trip to the health food store followed by The Ruler's gas-producing lentil soup and her two-ton rosemary bread. Not.

But there is one good thing about going to the Nut 'n' Nut. I look all hopeful at The Ruler.

"Absolutely, Sherry," she says, reading my mind. "We'll make sure you get to browse the clothes at the Rack."

Back in the kitchen, Grandma's rinsing out her bowl. "You're safe now. The house was very receptive." She beams at all of us. "I'm going home to set out sunflower seeds for one of my wrens."

"Thanks for all your help," The Ruler says.

"My pleasure. Nothing I like better than sharing my spiritual talents." Grandma drops a kiss on Sam's forehead, then mine. She gives The Ruler an iron-strong hug. "You've got nothing to worry about." And she clomps out the door.

I wish I believed all my problems in life could be solved with a bowl of burnt cloves + salt.

But I don't. No, I believe my future is crammed with problems. Problems way too serious to be solved with any combo of herbs and seasonings.

chapter
fourteen

It's Sunday morning. The Ruler pokes her head into the pantry. With everything labeled, she can tell at a glance what ingredients she's missing. She calls out a list for me to jot down. I've never even heard of half the stuff, which is making me nervous. I mean, how healthy can it be to eat things you can't spell?

The Ruler unhooks the reusable, dye-free cotton shopping bags and the key to Dad's car. And through the door we go, Sam patting his pocket to check for his video game, me tipping the end of a box of Nerds into my mouth and The Ruler sticking the grocery list into the front compartment of her ugly goes-with-everything black canvas purse.

Headed to the health food store, The Ruler's her

regular cautious-granny-driving self. One mile faster and she'd be at the speed limit. But, after the tire slashing, I'm glad to have some safety in my day.

We crawl into a parking space. "Why don't you catch up with us inside the Nut 'n' Nut, Sherry?" The Ruler says.

She doesn't have to ask twice. I'm unbuckled and on the sidewalk faster than you can say "new clothes." Because next door to the health food store is the Rack, one of the best, most reasonable, most fashionable clothing stores in Phoenix.

I beeline to the sale rack, located right inside the front door. It's tops week. I paw through the hangers. And, yay, there's a decent selection in extra-small. I choose a turquoise + sea green baby-doll that goes perfectly with my skin tone, my dark eyes, my dark hair, the walls of my bedroom and the gravel in my aquarium. I love a well-coordinated life. And what luck that I haven't blown all my allowance yet this month and can actually buy the top.

I flip over the tag. Two for one. Oh, happy days! I pick out a lilac blouse. After paying, I bolt next door to fulfill my bodyguard duties.

It's only when I'm inside the Nut 'n' Nut that I remember how my stomach goes all churny at this store's smell. Vitamins and onions and fish and skin cream should not be such close neighbors.

I catch up to The Ruler and Sam in the frozen food

section. The Ruler admires my purchases, which convinces me that I am slowly having a positive influence on her lack of fashion sense. Sam ignores me, frenziedly pressing buttons on his game. No matter. I am his sister and will be there for him when he needs my expert clothing advice.

"Can we get some soysicles?" Sam asks.

"Of course." The Ruler beams at him. She's determined to change the eating habits of the world, one by one.

She divides up the shopping list and sends me off for tomatoes, scallions and fresh rosemary.

Pushing a mini kid's cart with a green Customer-in-Training flag, I detour down the natural-candy aisle. I'm contemplating fake-o licorice, an item so not on my list, but quite tasty.

Suddenly, the cinnamony + sugary smell of a Cinnabon floats past me. I stand perfectly still.

It's Mrs. Howard.

The Cinnabon smell gets stronger and stronger, until the air is practically sticky.

I wait for her to say, "Hi, Sherry. How's the mystery going?" Or, "Cute outfit, love how you put your clothes together." Or, "The Academy really thinks you're marvelous and brilliant."

But no, silence.

And it hits me that she doesn't even know I know

she's there. She doesn't realize I can smell her. I can't see her blurry outline; she must have control over that. Mrs. Howard's spying on me.

Okeydokey, Mrs. Thinks-She's-So-Tricky-Invisible-Guidance-Counselor-Ghost Howard. I can get into this game. I hum a bland nothing tune. "Dum dee dee dum. Better hurry to the produce aisle for some deliciously fresh and healthy tomatoes and scallions and rosemary.

"Dum dee dee dum. I can't wait till the lentil soup is merrily bubbling away on our stove at home, filling our cozy kitchen with warmth and goodness.

"Dum dee dee dum. And I so hope I get to knead the bread. Because I'm a very helpful girl."

I'm all the while skipping along, zigzagging the cart so the Customer-in-Training flag flaps jauntily away.

At the vegetables, I tear off a plastic bag and drop in a couple of plump tomatoes. I'm tossing scallions and rosemary up into the air when, *poof,* the Cinnabon smell is gone. I smile. I gold-starred that Academy of Spirits test.

It's a manic roll over to the bulk bins where The Ruler and Sam are scoring lentils.

Sam's scooping up the beans. The Ruler's picking out the bad ones, prodding them back into the bin with these bamboo tweezer thingies. They're joking around, laughing. The Ruler's beige blouse has come untucked and she's letting it hang there. I'm kind of not surprised they're having fun; Sam can make anything into a game.

So I bodyguard the rest of Sunday morning, which drifts into the afternoon. By which time, I seriously need a nap. The woman never slows down. We clean. We cook. We bake. We garden. We shop at a specialty store for canning supplies.

It's all worth it because I'm sure my mother is taking advantage of her nonbodyguarding time and practicing up a storm for the Ghostlympics.

Finally, finally, with heavy eyelids, I head to my room for some downtime. One step in and I'm getting a happy feeling. Thanks to Grandma's clove mixture, my room smells fun and holidayish, like the Christmas store at the mall. I wander over to my aquarium 'cause I want a palsy-walsy chat with my adorable bala sharks before taking a nap.

Yikes. There's fish food floating in the water. Which there should not be because I fed them yesterday. And they so don't need food again today. They'll get sick.

Shoulders back and a glare on my face, I storm into Sam's room. "How many times do I have to tell you to leave my fish alone? Don't feed them. You'll kill them and I'll never forgive you."

He's in a beanbag chair, thumbs flapping furiously over his controller. He doesn't even look up. "I didn't feed your stupid fish."

"I can tell you've been in my room. You left behind your gross dirty-sock smell. So don't even bother lying." I slam his door on the way out. Back in my room, I scoop out as much of the flakes as I can with a little aquarium net.

I flop down on my bed. I shut my eyes. I haven't craved a nap this bad since last weekend.

Ding-dong.

I drag my weary self to the front door.

It's Junie.

She's surprise-visiting to help me with the Donner Dynamos' website stuff. Ixnay on the nap.

In the kitchen, we nuke ham-and-cheese Hot Pockets. I'm bringing Junie up to speed on the mystery since she wasn't at the meeting with Mom and Grandpa. I tell her about the Ghostlympics.

"Where would you spend five minutes of Real Time with your mom?" Junie asks.

"I can't decide." I set down my Hot Pocket. "Not anywhere public, not even Tio Roberto's, because I don't want it to be noisy. I haven't seen her for over a year and a half, and I want to hear every word she says." I actually tear up.

"Sherry, I really hope she wins Real Time," Junie says.

Then we both sit in sadness and silence for a minute.

I pick up my Hot Pocket and nibble. "We better eat

lunch near Kyle and his friends tomorrow. Maybe we'll overhear something."

"Oh great." Junie sighs. "Lunch by the cool eighth graders. Who don't want us around."

We're walking down the hall to the office, totally side by side, shoulders touching. Junie says, "What about the Donner robotics team? Are any of those students crazy enough to slash The Ruler's tires?"

"Oh yeah," I say. "They're way, way out there. And we have no idea what their secret plans are. Maybe plan A was to slash the front tires, and plan B was to slash the rear tires."

Then I pause, trying to make sure I say the next thing right. Because Junie can be overly sensitive. "Are most students in robotics clubs wacked-out weirdos?"

Junie hmpfs and speeds up so she's a step ahead and showing me her back. "Sherry, don't be such a moron."

In the office, I switch on the computer. "Anyway, someone from the Donner Dynamos could definitely be doubling as a tire slasher, like Claire. Or maybe it was Kyle the Flunking Basketball Player. Or maybe Kyle's dad. Or maybe it's someone we don't even know about."

I log on to my e-mail. "I sent a short, friendly questionnaire to the Donner team members. Most of them have e-mailed me back with their answers. And a photo. If you could just paste everything onto the Web pages."

"Uh, why?" Junie asks, her face puzzled. "Why are you trying to help Donner win?"

chapter
fifteen

"**I**'m not trying to help Donner win, Junie. But we haven't ruled them out as suspects yet," I explain slowly, like I'm talking to a preschooler. "I want to go to more of their meetings to keep track of them. Which means I've gotta walk the walk and talk the talk, like I'm truly a Donner Dynamo."

Junie rolls her eyes.

I open an e-mail from Sarah.

Junie scans it. "Uh, Sherry, this isn't the kind of stuff you normally put on a robotics club website. Normally, on the members page, it's information about where they plan to go to high school and college, how long they've been involved with robotics, their position on the team." She looks back at the e-mail. "Not, uh, personal stuff, like favorite childhood toy, favorite vacation, most embarrassing moment."

"Well, they put me in charge of the questionnaire, and that's the way I'm doing it."

Junie harrumphs like an old lady, but starts copying and pasting and uploading anyway. She knows that once I make my mind up, there's pretty much no changing it. Anyway, it's not her team.

I push my chair back to go get a Mountain Dew.

Junie lifts her hands off the keyboard. "Don't you think I should be showing you how to do this?"

"Uh, no. I'm not actually on the Donner robotics team," I explain überpatiently.

"Uh, Sherry, I'm not either."

"Fine." I scoot back up to the computer. "Show me."

When she's done with Mohawk Guy's page, I say, "Let me try the next one. You get the sodas."

"Works for me." Junie heads for the kitchen.

I click on Austin's e-mail. And start reading. And stop.

Junie comes back and sits down next to me and pops open both our cans. "What's going on? You hit a snag?"

"Not a snag. It's this e-mail from Austin, one of the Donner guys."

She squints at the screen. " 'Mary, we're so thrilled to have you as our most recent Donner Dynamo team member. Please call me if there's anything I can help you with.'"

Junie and I stare at each other, then say at the exact same sec, "Plan A and plan B!"

I pull my cell out of my pocket and punch in Austin's number.

"Hi, Austin. It's, uh, Mary. I just opened your e-mail."

"Hi, Mary. Did you love your first Donner Dynamos meeting? Isn't robotics amazing? Thanks for joining the Dynamos. How're the Web pages going? Do you need any help?"

"Nope. They're fine. Really fine."

"You're a great addition to our team. I have a good feeling about you."

Guilt! Since I'm only doing a good job so the Donner Dynamos will accept me and let me snoop at their meetings. "Uh, thanks."

Junie pokes me in the side. "Ask him about the plans."

"Hey, Austin, I'm feeling kind of left out and in the dark about plan A," I say, setting the phone on the desk so Junie can hear too.

And he starts babbling like a little kid after too much birthday cake. "Plan A is we're going to seriously spy on Saguaro's bot. We'll start at the practice competition at Emerson Middle School on Monday evening. With our phone cameras and video cameras and notebooks. And we'll post someone at Emerson every afternoon and weekend when the practice fields are open for just regular old practice time. We'll figure out their bot's weaknesses. And we'll watch to see their drivers' strategies. Like are they going for points by racing around the field, or are they knocking the other team's ball out, or are they concentrating on moving the ball around? Once we know their strategies, we'll tweak ours to beat them." He's talking very speedy. The flash drive must be pretty much break-dancing around his neck.

Junie mouths, "So?"

I lean over and speak into the phone. "Austin, doesn't everyone kind of do that?"

"Not to the same degree. Also, and here's the clincher, we'll give the info to every team that goes up against Saguaro. So everyone has an edge on them."

Junie's eyebrows leap way up by her hairline.

"Very brainy," I say. "So, tell me about plan B."

"You know what, Mary?" Austin pauses. "That's more Claire's department."

chapter
sixteen

The Ruler's at the stove, sterilizing the canning lids by dropping them into a pot of boiling water. "How's the homework going with Junie?"

"Good." I grab a tube of Pringles and a bag of sour Gummi Worms.

She actually whole-body-winces at my snack choice, but doesn't say anything. To her credit, she puts those snacks on her shopping list. 'Cause she knows they make me happy.

The Ruler turns back to the pot and tongs out the lids, one by one, and lays them to dry on a paper towel.

The open dishwasher shows off its army of glass mason jars, all clean and dry, standing at attention in the top rack. And on the counter, there are about three thousand pounds of cucumbers and four thousand piles of tomatoes.

I'm super thrilled to not be involved with the canning torture. I'm super, super thrilled to know The Ruler will be busy and safe in our kitchen all night, which means I'll get a bodyguarding break. I'm super, super, super thrilled to be meeting Josh at Jazzed-Up Juice tonight. Josh Morton. Just thinking his name turns my insides to an oatmealy mush.

"I'm about ready for your brother." The Ruler sets a pile of labels and a marker next to the lids.

"Looks like you guys'll be canning till, like, Thanksgiving."

"We probably could." The Ruler smiles. "But I figure Sam will only last an hour, two tops. After that, we might go to the mall for a movie."

To the mall? As in, outside in the dangerous stalker-filled world? In order for me to go to Jazzed-Up Juice with Josh, I need The Ruler to totally stay put, here in our safe and sound suburban house. "For an excellent canning job, you should do the whole entire thing. Every tomato. Every cucumber."

The Ruler's back is to me while she's working at the sink, running water over cucumbers. "We're not canning the cukes tonight. Just soaking them in pickle brine."

"Sam has amazing staying power. He could easily

go ten, twelve hours without a break. Definitely do all the tomatoes, okay?"

She picks up a brush and starts scrubbing the cucumbers. "Are you planning to help?"

"Uh, no. Remember I'm going out with Josh?"

"Well then, Sam and I will stop after a couple of hours. We might go out. We might not."

I full-throttle it to the office.

When I get there, Junie's tap-tapping on the keyboard, still uploading Donner Web stuff.

I pop the lid on the Pringles and pass her the container.

Junie pulls out a couple of chips and munches away.

"Interested in going to the movies tonight?" I say.

"Maybe. Which one?" She plunks the container on the desk.

I take a chip. "Something G-rated."

"G-rated?"

"With Sam and The Ruler." I hold out the sour Gummi Worms to her.

"No thanks and no thanks."

"Puhleeze, Junie," I whine. "Turns out they're only canning for a couple of hours. And then they might go to the movies. Where she'll need to be bodyguarded. But I'll be out with Josh."

"See if you can get together with Josh now," Junie says calmly.

"And you'll keep working on the website?"

"Just for a while." Junie's cell beeps with a text. She flips open the phone, reads the message and smiles. "Actually, I think I'm done working on the Donner site."

I grab her phone. "Nerdy Nick? You're getting texts from Nerdy Nick?"

Her face and neck are the color of red Skittles.

I read the message aloud. " 'I'm free. How bout u?' "

And while I'm in my shocked shock that Junie's texting with Nerdy Nick about chilling together, she very easily stretches out an arm like Cat Woman and plucks her phone from my hand.

I shake my head to clear out the craziness lurking there. "It's for robotics, right? You do not *even* want to know what I was thinking. That you and Nerdy Nick . . ."

She doesn't dignify my craziness with an answer, just lets her thumbs tap-dance over her phone's keypad. Then she stands and seizes her purse.

"But my Jazzed-Up Juice date with Josh . . ."

Junie grabs her Mountain Dew and flashes me a quick smile. "See ya."

I take a deep breath and speed-dial the love of my life.

"Hey, Sherry," Josh says. "What's up?"

"Messing around on the computer. What're you doing?"

"Still working on English with Candy."

"Can you be done? Because I'm free now."

"Let me ask." His voice fades, but I can still hear him. "It's Sherry. She wants to meet now." There's a short pause while he listens. "Oh, okay." He clears his throat. "Uh, Sherry, I guess not."

"Oh," I say from the depths of my flip-flops. "The Ruler and Sam might go to a movie later."

"And we can't be alone in your house."

And I have to protect The Ruler from a crazy stalker. "But they might not go. They haven't decided yet."

"Hey," Josh says, "I have a great idea." And he tells me.

I get off the phone and finish up the Donner member pages. And the Pringles. And my Mountain Dew. Then I change into jean capris and my new, lilac blouse from the Rack. I restraighten my hair and redo my eye makeup. I'm just applying the eleventh and final coat of gloss on my visibly plumper lips, when the doorbell rings.

My skin tingles. I know it's Josh. Because we are so on the same page.

From the top of the stairs, I peer over the banister as Sam dashes to the door and swings it wide open. "Josh! Dude! Are those for us?"

Yuppers. That very fine boyfriend of mine has arrived, swinging a cardboard drink carrier with four drinks from Jazzed-Up Juices. And poking out of his pocket is a rented video game.

Our plan: to make sure The Ruler and Sam stay home.

"Hey, Sam." Josh sets down the carrier and waves the video game in the air. "You up for this?"

Sam goes bug-eyed. He loves to chill with Josh. And he loves *Super Go-Kart*. The Ruler couldn't drag him from the house tonight.

The three of us hang in the living room, playing. Eventually, The Ruler calls Sam into the kitchen to finish up with the canning.

Josh scoots next to me, right next to me. Our legs touch from the hip down. My nerve endings throw off flames. When he drapes an arm over my shoulder, I pretty much melt into him. Because we've been together for two whole wonderful months, I can read his moves.

So when Josh's head inclines the teeniest bit to the side, I know his lips are headed for mine. Then it's like I'm on autopilot, like we're just programmed to be excellent kissers. My head does a complementary dip.

And we do kiss.

And it is great.

But somehow even in the awesome moment of it, my mind is wandering.

chapter
seventeen

It's Monday at lunch and I'm cranky.

Cool people are not in their right minds. At least not the cool people at my school who insist on sitting at the *outside* lunch tables. Why? We have a perfectly good cafeteria *inside* where it's air-conditioned and, uh, cool. But, no, they choose to eat out here in a climate similar to that of Mercury. Which, for some strange reason, I happen to know has temperatures of around six hundred degrees Fahrenheit. Cool people must spend all their allowance on deodorant.

Kyle, whom I'm supposed to be spying on, hasn't shown up. Junie, who's supposed to be spying with me, hasn't shown up either.

I'm squished at the table next to where Kyle and

his gang chill, trying desperately to hang on to space for me and Junie. This is not as easy as it sounds, because, apparently, I'm invisible to eighth-grade girls, who keep edging me out. Hello, people! I'm here. I exist. I'm just one year younger.

On top of my territory troubles, I've got Ghostlympic worries. Today's the preliminaries. Mom has to make it through this round or Real Time is out the window. And now that I know about Real Time, my intestines are all tight and braided up because I want those five minutes with her more than anything else in the world.

There's a lentil-sized legume of guilt niggling me about Real Time and Sam. He doesn't even get to connect with Mom the way I do for the mystery solving. He doesn't get to connect with her at all. But every time I think of giving him the Real Time, if Mom even wins it, I realize how bad I want to see her.

"Could ya give me some room here?" says an eighth-grade girl with hoop earrings the size of Frisbees.

I slide a fraction of an inch.

Earring Girl squeezes in, barely, between me and an eighth-grade girl with long brown hair and a thick, flowery hair band. I'm surrounded by squealing, yakking cool girls and their lunch trays. Because they all bought. Because, as everyone knows, buying is the cool thing to do.

From a brown paper bag, I pull out a tuna sandwich on whole wheat. Tuna mixed with some of The Ruler's newly canned relish. Which, surprisingly, is actually very delish. I'm even getting used to the grainy bread.

Every few sentences, the girls toss me a what-are-you-doing-here? look. I just ignore them. Seriously, this *is* a public middle school.

"Troy Garcia asked me out," Hair Band Girl says.

Three girls scream.

"To Rollerblade World," she continues. "But I'm so bummed. I totally need a new top. But I'm so broke."

I can relate to that.

"Sucks." Earring Girl unwraps a sandwich on blindingly white bread. She obviously has no sense of dietary fiber.

"You wanna borrow something from my closet?" asks a blonde dressed in shades of pink.

Hair Band Girl frowns. "But our colors are so different."

Once again, I can relate. You try being BFF with a redhead like Junie. It totally nixes clothes trading. Plus, she's a bigger size than me.

Speaking of which, where is that girl? I pull out my cell and text.

Me: where r u?
Junie: robotics emergency.

Me: ur supposed to be spying on kyle
with me.
Junie: robotics emergency.
Me: wut abt the mystery?
Junie: gotta go. robotics emergency.

"How much money do you have?" asks a girl who's breaking the school dress code by wearing a tank top.

Hair Band Girl sighs out a depressingly low number.

And I'm relating again. Because living fashionably on my allowance takes skill and talent. And a lot of sales.

"That sucks," Earring Girl says.

They all take bites of their matching spongy white-bread sandwiches. Hair Band Girl looks miserable.

I have no idea why I leap into the conversation. "Have you checked out the clothes at the Rack?"

The girls turn and stare at me with their shadowed, outlined, mascaraed beautiful eyes.

"Who are you?" Pink Girl says.

"Sherry Baldwin."

"She's a seventh grader." Earring Girl returns to her nibbling.

"Aren't you Josh Morton's girlfriend?" Hair Band Girl says.

I tear open a package of low-sodium, low-fat baked fake-o Cheetos. "Yeah."

And their hostility evaporates into the stifling,

make-your-face-shiny Phoenix air. Which, quite frankly, is überbogus. Because I'm still a seventh grader.

"What's the Rack?" Hair Band Girl says. "I've never heard of it."

The others shake their heads.

"The Rack? It's next to the Nut 'n' Nut? The health food store downtown?" I tweezer out a fake-o Cheeto. "It's this smallish store that pretty much always has a sale rack going. Anyway, they have incredible prices."

They all stop chewing.

"Right now, they have this great sale on tops. Thirty percent off the sale price and buy one, get one free." I gnaw on the Cheeto. "I'm not entirely sure how you figure out the final price," I say to Hair Band Girl, "but I'm guessing you've got enough."

"You get that top there?" She points to my turquoise + sea green baby-doll.

I smooth it out. "As a matter of fact," I say proudly.

And when I tell them the price, there's a group jaw drop. This is followed by a group silence while they all mull over how much money they have in their cool, eighth-grade purses.

"Wow. Thanks, Josh's Girlfriend." Hair Band Girl's got a big grin going.

"The name's Sherry."

"Then thanks, Sherry."

And while I'm taking a slug of fluoridated bottled

water, she leans over and plucks a pretend Cheeto from my bag.

"Try not to think of it as a Cheeto," I say. "More as a paper substitute."

She gently scoots it under her napkin.

"Hey, do you guys happen to know where Kyle is?" I say.

"You're interested in him now too?" Earring Girl asks. "Aren't there *any* decent guys in your grade?"

"I'm not interested in him that way." I toss the bag of fake-o Cheetos in the nearby trash. "I have a few questions."

Hair Band Girl laughs. "If you've been toilet-papered, it was Kyle."

"Kyle is so wild and crazy." Pink Girl gives a little shake, like she's shivering.

"Kyle's done with wild and crazy for a while," Earring Girl says. "He has in-school suspension for all this week. And his dad grounded him last week. No sports, no friends, no TV. Until he raises his grades."

"I heard his math tutor picks him up from school and takes him directly home," Hair Band Girl says.

"And the math tutor leaves when the Spanish tutor arrives. Kyle won't see the sun for weeks." Earring Girl shakes her head so hard in sympathy that her hoops smack against her cheeks. "His stepmom plays bunco with my mom, so I get all the Kyle scoop."

Certainly doesn't sound like Kyle did the tire slashing. He's too heavily guarded by tutors. Another dead-end lead.

I sure hope Mom or Grandpa discovers something. Like when Mom's at the district board meeting today. Maybe a crazed math teacher wants the department head job big-time bad, and he's freaking The Ruler so she'll drop out of the running. Or maybe when Grandpa's shadowing Kyle's dad, he'll dig up something concrete.

"You know who I feel really sorry for?" Earring Girl says, not looking sorry at all. "Kyle's math teacher."

"Why?" My elbows on the table, I lean in close.

"He's got some major evil planned for her once he's off restriction."

chapter
eighteen

"Wow! Mom, that's fantastic!" It's after school, and I'm with Mom and Grandpa on our back porch. The Ruler's still at school, having a last-minute robotics meeting before tonight's practice competition. Junie's there too, of course. Sam's at Little League. Mom is spilling all the cool details about the Ghostlympics.

"What'd you have to get them to do?" I ask.

"Pick up small objects, like buttons and Legos." Mom's voice is giddy with pride. "And there were animals I'd never experimented with before: a veiled chameleon, a hamster. . . ."

"Your mom was *magnifico*." Grandpa lifts a spindly

leg to his beak and blows a kiss Hollywood-style. "Truly magnifico."

I actually understood him. At least I'm pretty sure I did. "Yay, Mom!"

"Sherry, what if I manage to pull this off? What if I win Real Time for us? I was thinking maybe we could get a soft pretzel together. We used to love that."

I imagine the two of us side by side on a bench at the mall, chewing and talking, warm pretzels in our hands. "Yeah, yeah, that'd be so great! What happens next at the Ghostlympics?"

"Tougher tasks. In the semifinals we have to get animals with bigger brains to move larger objects." The cushion on the garden chair where my mom's sitting gives a little shake. "It's much more complicated."

Sounds very robotics-ish. "When are the semifinals?"

"They start tonight at six. And they'll last for hours."

I freeze. "But tonight's the robotics practice competition." I start twirling my hair. "Can Grandpa come with me?"

"No," he squawks.

"Your grandfather's a runner again at the Ghostlympics," Mom says. "Besides, no one's going to let a bird fly around inside at a robotics meet."

"Wait a sec. I might not even have to go to the

practice competition, right?" I untangle my finger. "What'd you find out at the district school board meeting, Mom?"

She sighs heavily. "Nothing of interest. A handful of math teachers applied for the department head position at Saguaro. Most of them have more experience than Paula, so she's not really a contender."

"Oh." I'm twirling my hair again. "What about you, Grandpa? Did you find out anything about Kyle's dad? Did he slash the tires?"

Grandpa shakes his little bird head. "Alibi."

I'm twirling my hair faster and faster, like it's a race. "Yeah, but he could've paid someone else to slash them."

He shakes his head again. "Doubtful."

"What about Kyle?" Mom asks.

"That's a big fat zero." I give them the details. "Although he does plan to give our house his deluxe TP treatment, which involves a ninety-six pack of toilet paper plus plastic forks stuck in the ground all over the front yard plus Saran Wrap around The Ruler's car."

"Sherry, you have to go to the robotics competition," Mom says softly. "To follow up on this lead and keep an eye on Paula. As best you can."

I bury my head in my hands. "The Donner team will be there wanting me to spy on my school. My school team will be there wanting me to be supportive. And if those fanatical Donner weirdos figure out not only do I go to Saguaro, but The Ruler is my stepmother . . ." I massage my head. "But no way I want you to quit the Ghostlympics and go with me."

Total and complete silence. Like the world has stopped spinning. Even Grandpa doesn't croak out anything.

I do *not* want my mom to ditch the Ghostlympics. Not in a million years. I want her to go to the semifinals, and ace them. I want her to advance to the finals where she blows everyone out of the water and wins Real Time. I'm not exactly sure what we'll use the five minutes on. But I know one thing—I'm getting a hug.

Which means I will be on my own at Emerson Middle School this evening. I suck in a deep detective breath. I will be on my sneakiest, sleuthiest, stealthiest behavior. I won't get caught by Donner. I won't get caught by Saguaro.

Because getting caught would be überbad.

After Mom and Grandpa take off, I sprawl out in the garden chair on the porch, trying to chill. From my head to my toes, I'm basically a bundle of anxious, jumpy nerves. The chilling business? It's not working.

My cell rings. "You're the Best" by the Boyfriends! Josh's song! I flip it open. "Hi, Josh."

"Hi, Sherry. What're you doing?"

"Chillin'."

"Guess what? I've got some great news."

Okay. Can I just say how much I love it when Josh gets all bubbly like a little kid at Chuck E. Cheese's? "What?"

"I scored us free movie tickets. From a customer at my mom's shop."

"Josh, you rock!"

"And that's not even the best part."

He is so beyond cute in his excitement. "What's the best part?"

"They're for *Janus*."

I squeal. *Janus*. Supposedly the chick flick to end all chick flicks. And my fine boyfriend will go with me.

"And that's not even the best part."

"What is the best part?"

"The tickets include popcorn and soda."

"Yay!"

"And that's not even the best part."

While it's definitely adorable when he's all bubbly and excited, it also gets old. "Seriously. What is the best part?"

"The tickets are for opening night."

"Isn't that tonight?" Which means the "best part" is rapidly morphing into the "worst part" for me.

"At six."

Does everything of consequence in Phoenix start

tonight at six o'clock? "I'm really, really sorry, but I can't go. I promised I'd go to this robotics thing."

"Bummer." He sounds like I popped his birthday balloon. "I don't want to just waste the tickets."

"Your mom?"

"Nah, she's already got tickets."

"Eric?" Even as the name leaves my lips, I know it's not going to work.

Josh snorts. "Eric's not into chick flicks. There'd have to be explosives and chase scenes."

And then a name pops into my mind. The name of someone who *is* into chick flicks. The name of someone who would Superwoman-vault over tall buildings in a single bound. Or break a chunky leg trying if it meant a chance to go out with Josh.

I hold my breath and just hope "Candy" doesn't leap from my mind over to Josh's.

After I get off the phone, I can't even sit still, I'm so antsy and full of worries. A horrible thought keeps replaying in my troubled mind. Josh and Candy will end up at *Janus* together.

Finally, I decide I can't take the torture for one more second.

I dig Polly's business card out of my purse.

"Hi, Polly," I say when she picks up.

"Hi, Sherry. What's up?"

"Remember that guy you said is really into me? The one with messy hair? Any chance he goes to the

137

movies with the glittery girl you saw talking to him? You know, during my reading."

"I couldn't say," Polly answers. "Maybe if I did a reading for one of them, I'd see something about a movie. But I might not. I sort of just see what I see. Why?"

"He has *Janus* tickets for tonight."

"Very cool."

"He asked me and all, but I can't go. So I was wondering if he asks her."

"It's just like I told you, Sherry, he really likes you. Even if he ends up going to *Janus* with the other girl, you don't need to worry."

Easy for her to say.

"What happened with the slashed tires?" Polly asks.

"The police think it was maybe teens or an unhappy student. My stepmom's a teacher."

"I had some scary vibes about her. Did you tell her to be way careful?"

"Uh, not yet."

"You should." Polly pauses. "You got a science test coming up?"

"Uh, yeah. As a matter of fact, I do. Worth half my grade."

"You better study."

You don't need to be a psychic to tell me that.

chapter
nineteen

I'm standing outside the door of Emerson's gym, looking in. Nervously. My eye is twitching like a camera shutter set on sports speed.

There are a gazillion middle-school students, parents, teachers, judges. Stick me in there and it'll be a gazillion and one. That's a lot of bodies. One body can hide and eavesdrop in the middle of a lot of bodies. I might actually be able to pull off this undercover operation. My eye twitch slows down.

I step in. It's noisy. Just as you would expect with all those bodies. It's hot. Just as you would expect with all those bodies.

There's a big box of safety glasses with a sign: SAFETY GOGGLES MUST BE WORN IN THE PIT. I strap on a pair. It's a disguise of sorts. This mission is doable. My eye twitch disappears.

The gym is divided in half. One half is a big rectangle with a two-foot-high Plexiglas fence around it. The field where the bots compete. The other half is divided into three rows. Each row is made up of about twelve team booths, six on each side of the row. The booths are constructed of plastic pipes and decorated with team banners and homemade posters. Inside most booths is a bunch of people with screwdrivers and drills, poking and prodding their robot. At the front of each booth, there's a basket of free team buttons.

Head ducked, I lurk at the end of each row, peering through the crowds to find the Donner booth. I need to sneak into the back of their stall before anyone from my school sees and identifies me. I figure I'll hide there for the evening, listening for any plans about The Ruler.

"Mary, finally, you're here."

With a scream, I jump.

"We've been looking for you." Claire's right in my face. With her shiny black hair totally straightened, the long side looks longer and the short side looks shorter. Add in a white and turquoise tie-dye T-shirt with a blazing fireball on the back and DONNER DYNAMOS in black letters across the front. Claire's got a real robotic-warrior thing going. "Where's your team shirt, Mary?"

"Dirty laundry," I mumble. I'm in jeans and a pastel pink blouse. Why? Because pink isn't a Donner school color, and pink isn't a Saguaro school color. Plus, pink goes well with my skin tone.

Claire frowns. "Here's the schedule I've made up for everyone." She pulls a sheet off her clipboard and hands it to me. "Your responsibilities are highlighted. And there's a note to remind you to bring the bling to our next meeting. We'll glue it on before we crate our bot."

I read the sheet. The eye twitch makes a comeback. "Claire, why am I mostly in the Saguaro booth? On spy duty."

"That's plan A," Claire says smugly.

I throw my hands up in the air. "But I'm over there more than anybody else. By a bunch."

"You're new to the Donner Dynamos. Judges are visiting the booths. They have the right to ask any team member any question. And we get judged on the answer." She flips the longer side of her hair back and it gleams under the fluorescent lights. "Imagine if they asked you a question?"

I glance back down at the paper. "What exactly is 'driving time' anyway? 'Cause that's what you scheduled yourself for."

"The driver handles the controls. So I'll be manning the remote that maneuvers our bot during the actual competition. I have the most experience driving. If you're interested, you can try that position next year."

Next year, schmext year. I want to grab her clipboard and whack her over the head with it. Repeatedly.

Claire points across the room. "The Saguaro Cacti are the next row over. They're number 9141. We're down this row. See our sign?"

"Yeah." I can definitely see their lame-o posterboard sign with team photos glued on in a circle around a hand-drawn fireball.

She glances at her watch. "You better head over now to the Saguaro booth. Bryce'll show you what to do. Don't leave till Austin gets there. He's your relief." She fiddles with the clip, making sure the remaining papers are secure. "Mary, does your cell have a decent camera?"

I'm walking away and nodding. After a few steps, I veer off to the opposite side of the room. I can so not kick it at the Saguaro booth with Bryce.

I hang out by the fence surrounding the field, sort of watching the competitions. There are four bots in the field at a time, working together in pairs. You drive your bot around the field, sometimes even racing. You pick up plastic rings and drop them on these peg thingies. You can even remove rings your opponents put on. It's all about getting points. There's lots of cheering. A noisy buzzer blares when the match is over. The sound system starts up, blasting loud music.

Under different circumstances, it might be fun. But not this evening. In my mind, I've pretty much gone over all the angles, and I'm blowing this pop stand. I can't chill with the Saguaro team because they'll out me to Bryce. I can't chill with the Donner team because Claire'll just send me over to the Saguaro booth. So I can't investigate. So I'm leaving. A good detective knows when to cut her losses and head home to finish her homework and catch some TV.

I should've gone to the movies with Josh. Instead he might actually be there with Candy. Hopefully, Polly Paulson knows her psychic stuff. I briefly squeeze my eyes shut. Not thinking about relationships right now. I just want out of here.

Hunched over and my chin leaning on my chest, I slink along the Plexiglas fence around the field toward the outside door. I'm totally focused on that door, my exit to freedom. And safety.

"Sherry! What a marvelous surprise," The Ruler says, all bright and cheerful and full of competitive energy. She's striding along in front of the Saguaro Cacti dolly + robot. Behind her is the entire team.

A sea of purple, yellow and black T-shirts with a cartoony robot cactus on the front.

Yikeserama!

"How wonderful of you to come to support us." Beaming, The Ruler turns toward her team. "Isn't this great? We have our first groupie."

Everything feels all slow-motiony, even my eye twitch. All buddy-buddy, Junie and Nerdy Nick are pushing the back of the dolly. Junie shoots me worried looks. Tongue-Stud Girl marches at one side, a tool belt clanking around her skinny waist. Honor Roll Girl marches on the other side, intent on her calculator.

No Bryce. A faint flicker of hope ignites in my chest. If I can make it to the exit . . .

The Saguaro Cacti join the lineup to check in for field time. Honor Roll Girl lags behind, frowning at her calculator. I inch, ever so slowly, like I'm in Jell-O, toward the door.

"Sherry." The Ruler hands me her clipboard. "Hold this for a second, would you?"

Bryce jack-in-the-box pops up from behind a huge gray trash can.

I freeze, my back up against the Plexiglas. A sitting duck.

He points his phone straight at me. *Click!*

My mind is totally blank. Like I'm taking a math

test. I can't think of a single way to salvage the situation.

The Ruler finishes tinkering with the robot's arm, then takes back her clipboard. "Thank you."

Bryce skulks up to Honor Roll Girl. "Do you know her?" he asks, giving me a suspicious glare.

Honor Roll Girl doesn't even meet his eyes, just keeps on punching long strings of numbers into her calculator. She delivers my death sentence. "Uh, Sherry Baldwin. She goes to our school. Ms. Paulson's her stepmother."

chapter
twenty

Those crazy Donner Dynamos totally freaked. Like when you kick over an anthill and the entire colony scrambles all chaotic and panicked.

In a calm, reasonable voice, I explained to them I would just ride home on my bike. I would not sabotage their bot. I would not talk to any judges. I would not even think one single robotic thought.

But, alas, the Donner Dynamos were all ants in their pants with Claire furiously flipping the long side of her hair back and forth and stomping around the booth. The others glared hot anger in my direction.

But it was Austin I felt the worst about. Austin, whose eyes usually sparkle with excitement for everything robotics, stared past me with a lackluster gaze.

When I tried to apologize, he turned away. His flash drive hung still and lifeless around his neck.

Bryce got his big brother to drive me out to nowheresville in the desert so that by the time I walked back to town, the competition would be over.

I look around. It's me, a bunch of saguaro cacti, scraggly bushes and tumbleweeds. The Arizona desert is not pretty. At least it's May, and there's still daylight.

From my backpack, I pull out the bottle of water Sarah gave me. I drink. I swallow. I think. This is the most bizarro mystery. Not that I have masses of experience, but still, absolutely nothing makes sense. Nothing. We don't have one solid suspect.

I flip open my phone to call Grandma.

Ack. No cell service.

I'm sitting there, sipping away and minding my own business, when a tumbleweed starts rolling in my direction. Yikes. I jump up and sidle left, out of its path. It slows, turns, then veers left. I jog to the right. It loops right. It's coming right at me, like I'm magnetized or something. I turn my back.

Whack. Whack. Whack.

Ouchie mama.

Suddenly, the crazed tumbleweed stops and just squats, like a giant pimple. There's no breeze. What set it in motion? I sniff. There's a faint odor of honey + dirty socks. So not a tumbleweedish smell.

Just as I raise the bottle to my mouth, it's ripped

from my hand. The bottle skitters across the dusty desert floor, droplets arcing through the air like a watery comet.

And then I fall. More like I'm pushed.

I go to stand. I'm shoved over again.

So there I am, lying on the hard-packed ground, cell phone serviceless, water bottleless, scratched up from a mean tumbleweed and surrounded by the yucky smell of honey + dirty socks. Something is way way wrong with the world.

"Stay out of robotics!" a raspy male voice shouts.

I leap to my feet and gaze around.

No one.

Not one single person.

Just me, a bunch of saguaro cacti and tumbleweeds. The stalker is a ghost!

chapter
twenty-one

Ack! Eek! Ike!

The stalker is a ghost!

A ghost who smells of honey + dirty socks!

I yank the ziplock bag of coffee beans from my purse. I grab a handful of beans and toss them high in the air. It's raining coffee beans. It's raining coffee smell. It's raining SOS signals to my mother.

"Mom!" I scream. "Mom! Mom!"

I flop on the hard desert floor, scrounging coffee beans off the ground and throwing them up in the air again. I'm thinking Mom thoughts. Desperate get-yourself-here-tout-de-suite Mom thoughts. As in, I'm beyond freaking out.

The tumbleweed is shaking. Then it's spinning on

the spot, like it's pawing the ground and gathering up energy to attack again. The honey + dirty socks odor is overpowering.

Just as the tumbleweed starts toward me, a super-strong coffee smell swishes in.

The honey + dirty socks smell disappears.

"Sherry! Sherry! Are you okay?"

"The stalker's a ghost, Mom! A ghost! He was here! But he's gone now!" I take a deep, raggedy breath and tell her everything.

When I'm done, she says, "We need off this case. It's too dangerous."

I used to freeze in the face of a challenge. Freeze up like a Popsicle. I couldn't move. Couldn't think. Couldn't speak.

But not anymore. Now I'm on top of my game.

I lean back on my elbows, legs stretched out, and shake my head. "I don't want off the case, Mom. I want this guy. If we quit now, it's like we're letting him win."

Mom's quiet. She's probably twirling her hair around her finger, thinking. "The fact that the stalker's a ghost certainly explains a lot, doesn't it?"

People used to always say how we looked alike, with our curly dark hair and dark eyes. I don't think they realized we had similar personalities too. I don't think I even realized it. But it feels excellent to be on track together.

"This ghost is talented," Mom says. "He picked up a *knife* and *slashed* tires. Ballpark guess, he's five levels ahead of me." She pauses. "I couldn't take it if something happened to you, Sherry."

"Would it help if I got an amethyst?" I ask, thinking back to the psychic fair.

"Yes, in the sense that the stone will break his concentration and make it tougher for him to approach you." She pauses. "Also, my presence and Grandpa's will chase him off. We can see him, and he doesn't want to be identified. The Academy has unpleasant ways of dealing with ghosts who harm the living."

My arms are misshapen with goose bumps the size of golf balls. But I know my mom will do everything in her power to keep me safe. "Okay. I'm getting amethysts for me and The Ruler and Junie. I won't go anywhere without coffee beans in my pocket, so I can call you the sec I smell him."

"Good plan," Mom says.

"The Ruler isn't so totally losing it after all. The ghost has been messing with her stuff. And he probably made those prank phone calls in the middle of the night." I stomp the ground, remembering the dirty sock smell in my room and how I'd blamed Sam. "I bet he sprinkled extra fish food in my aquarium." And that seals the deal. Because you mess with my fish, you are *definitely* messing with me.

"I am so annoyed," Mom and I say at the same time.

I jump up and start walking. "I gotta get outta here before the sun goes down."

"We'll talk with Mrs. Howard later," Mom says, blowing along beside me. "When the Ghostlympics are done for the day."

"The Ghostlympics!" I hit my forehead. "How'd you do?"

"I did well," she says slowly, "but I'm disqualified. I left in the middle of an event."

My stomach sinks to the desert floor, past the earth's crust, all the way to the core. "I wrecked our chances for Real Time. It's all I think about. How to spend those precious five minutes with you. And now they're gone."

Mom strokes my hair, so light and feathery I can barely feel it. "I think about them too. But calling me was the right thing, pumpkin. We'll try again next year."

Off in the distance, a tiny speck of dirt turns into a bigger speck of dirt, which turns into a flapping grandfather.

At the exact moment that Grandpa touches down on my slouched shoulder, the sweet scent of Cinnabon fills the air.

Mrs. Howard's vague roundish shape lingers above me like a low cloud as Mom does the report thing.

"The PSS assured us this mystery was straight-forward." Mrs. Howard shakes her head. "Had we known the stalker was a ghost, we wouldn't have assigned y'all the case. Far too risky. We'll reassign it immediately."

"No!" Mom and I shout together. "We can solve it."

"We're committed, Minnie May," Mom says. "It's personal for us."

"And me," Grandpa caws.

Mrs. Howard paces in front of me. About a foot off the ground. Finally, she says, "Fine. You can take a stab at it. I'll give you two days to wrap this case up. Any more time than that, and I'm worried the stalker will lose it like a treed raccoon and the entire situation will spiral out of control." Mrs. Howard runs pudgy sausage fingers through her hair. "Christine, there's an independent tutorial in the library called 'About Ghosts Who Don't Move On.' I suggest you review it tomorrow morning."

"Will do," Mom says.

Then, Mrs. Howard floats right in front of me. So close, the air is sickeningly sweet. "Sherry, honey, y'all were counting on Real Time?"

"Yeah, but I couldn't help it; I just freaked when the stalker turned out to be a ghost."

Mrs. Howard paces some more, then drifts to me again. "I understand how important Real Time is, particularly between a mother and daughter."

My eyes prickle with tears.

"Without going into great detail, I experienced a similar situation." Mrs. Howard's blurry hand covers her blurrier heart. "And, to this very day, I deeply regret the outcome."

I blink a bunch.

"I do believe the Academy is, in an oblique way, responsible for your mother's disqualification from the Ghostlympics." She draws in a breath. "Therefore, if you solve this mystery within the two-day period, we'll award you five minutes of Real Time."

We have another chance at Real Time!

"That means talking the stalker into the silver box at midnight on Wednesday." Her arms jiggle as she waves goodbye.

The sun's starting to set. Grandpa flies ahead to check on The Ruler. Mom and I keep traveling the dusty road back to town.

"The silver box is for ghosts who haven't moved on," Mom's explaining to me. "You somehow talk a ghost into the box and then deliver him to the Academy, who then moves him on."

I kick a stone and it skips ahead of us. "Why's he even hanging around?"

"There's a variety of reasons. Maybe he doesn't realize he's dead. Or he was too sad or angry at the time of death to be able to move on. Or he has unfinished business."

We catch up to the stone and I send it sailing again.

"You can't talk a ghost in without knowing his identity." Mom picks up the stone and lobs it. "Which is why I was saying earlier that the stalker won't want Grandpa or me to see him."

"So now we're tracking down a dead suspect," I say. "Like a dead student or teacher or parent who's peeved at The Ruler. Or a dead rival robotics person."

"Stalkers are often old boyfriends." Mom scoops up the stone and drops it in front of my foot.

I kick the stone high. "That's a lot of dead possibilities."

We discuss our plans of attack. Mom knows a fair amount about ghosts who don't move on, but the tutorial will teach her the very specific dot-your-i's-and-cross-your-t's rules for talking a ghost in.

It's dusky enough now that people are turning on lights, which twinkle friendly and happy to see me back safe and sound from my desert adventure.

My cell phone sings to let me know I've got messages. Which means, of course, that I've got service now.

Three people are hiking toward me. Two of them fill me with happiness. The other gives me the blahs.

chapter
twenty-two

"Hi, Junie! Hi, Josh!" I wave big. "Hi, Nick."

"You're okay now, with your friends?" Mom asks. "Because I want to find out the results of the semi-finals."

"I'm good." I wave her on.

She retrieves our stone, then zings it at a cactus. Bull's-eye.

Just like how we're going to nail this mystery.

The scent of coffee fades as Junie, Josh and Nerdy Nick start running toward me. I'd run too, but my feet are sore. Too much walking on uneven ground in inappropriate but cute footwear.

Josh sweeps me up in a big hug. Not the kind of hug you give your girlfriend if you're thinking about a certain overglittered eighth grader. Polly really might know what she's talking about. I inhale nice and deep. Nothing beats the essence of chlorine.

"Hey, you didn't go to *Janus*," I say from the depths of his chest.

"Nah, but I wish we'd gone together. Then this wouldn't have happened to you." Josh releases me and holds me out at arm's length. "Look at you. You're scraped up." He frowns, all mad. "I just wanna get those guys!"

"Yeah, well, except for the long walk part, the Donner kids weren't all that bad," I say. "Just easily panicked."

"What about this?" He traces the bruise on my arm.

"It's from my brother. An accident."

"What about all these scratches?"

"I tripped. A bunch. Plus, a tumbleweed blew into me." I can't mention the ghost-stalker. Academy rules. I'll fill Junie in later.

Josh frowns. Junie gives me a quick hug.

"Sherry's pretty uncoordinated," she says. "She was born that way."

Sorta kinda thank you, BFF. My hand reaches for Josh's and squeezes on. Then we start strolling back to civilization. "How'd you guys find me?"

"At the end of the competition," Junie says, "one of the Donner Dynamos, Sarah, hunted me down to tell me where they ditched you."

"Sarah's cool," I say.

"Nick recognized the road from her description"—Junie smiles at him—"and figured out how to get here by bus."

"Wow, Nick, that was pretty nice of you. Thanks." I like his change of attitude.

"I'm excellent with directions and public transportation," he says.

Improved attitude, but not too humble.

"Lucky for us." Junie's eyes twinkle at him. Then she skips to catch up to me and says quietly, "Are you really okay, Sherry? You look different somehow."

You'd look different too if you'd just been pushed around the desert by a ghost, then made your mind up to go head to spooky head with him. I'm probably maturing at a faster than average rate. "I'm good." Then I whisper, "We *have* to talk."

"Junie told me all about how you infiltrated the Donner team just to help our school win." Josh swings my arm big. "Way to go."

Good cover, Junie.

At the bus stop, the four of us hang together. I notice Junie's wearing pink lip liner and matching lipstick. The liner is definitely making her lips look thicker. Very chic. I pinch my bottom lip a few times, which is the best I can do at the moment.

The conversation swings to the practice competition.

"I really don't get it," Junie says. "Our robot is seriously superior to Donner's, but they outperformed us."

Nerdy Nick rubs his forehead, frowning. "A large part of Donner's troubles last year stemmed from their lack of leadership. This year, Claire Greene has stepped up to the plate and is successfully captaining the team."

"That's not what I'm talking about," Junie says. "Donner cost us points because their robot kept flipping our rings off the pegs."

"That's fair game," Nerdy Nick says.

Junie's forehead creases. "I know, but from where I was standing, I don't see how their robot was consistently successful. A couple of times, its arm looked like it was about an inch away from the ring."

"Optical illusion," Nerdy Nick says.

Honestly, the guy's got an answer for everything.

Her tongue pointing out between her teeth, Junie's pondering. "I guess that's it. I mean, what else could be the explanation?"

Optical illusion? Or ghost-stalker? That's where my mind's leaping.

Junie and Nerdy Nick launch into a whole boring discussion about engineering and robot parts and other überstrange topics. No surprise why these two aren't dating anyone yet.

Josh and I meander away from the bus stop to the

far side of a palm tree. We scooch in close and wrap our arms around each other. The sun is setting, going down behind a three-story building across the street. First, it sorta sits on top of the roof. Then it sinks down, like it's scratching itself on the gutter. We're both quiet. With Josh's arm around me and my head leaning against his chest, we're soaking up the romance of the moment. Just chilling on the same wavelength of love.

He tilts my head back and moves in for one of his signature Josh Morton kisses. I can't describe them; they're so magical. A mixture of orange Starburst candies + your stomach in the air when you speed down a steep hill on your bike + something fried. For a brief moment, my mind empties of mysteries and stalkers and ghosts and silver boxes.

We break apart and my mind instantly fills back up with mystery worries. Too bad Josh's kisses didn't have a more long-term effect. Like a suntan.

"Sherry," Junie calls. "Josh. The bus is coming."

We dash to the bus stop in time to hop up when the door wheezes open. The four of us trudge to the empty back where Josh and I squish into a seat together. Junie and Nerdy Nick sit behind us.

Josh flips open his phone and scans a text. "Candy and her friend really liked *Janus*."

So that's what he did with the tickets.

He reads more and groans. "I don't think I need

English tutoring again tomorrow." Without texting back, he shoves the phone in his pocket. "Dude, that girl is way intense."

I puff up with superiorness. No one has ever accused me of being intense over English.

Josh wrinkles his cute little freckled nose. "I'm starting The Ruler's after-school math tutorial sometime this week."

Like the way a dog perks up when he hears the word "bone" or "real-chicken treat," Nerdy Nick's all attention. "I have a math tutoring appointment with Kyle Rogers tomorrow morning before first period. Would you like to join us?"

"Cool." Josh is digging that. Anything to get out of spending extra time in a classroom. But has he thought about the equation of Nick + Kyle + Josh?

And what's up with Nerdy Nick? Is he tired of his loner-with-high-grades status? Or hoping to score extra cash? I shoot raised eyebrows at Junie, but she doesn't see me.

The Ruler phones to find out when I'm coming home. I tell her I'm on the way. I don't mention the whole ditched-in-the-desert thing. But her voice reminds me that I have questions about her past. "Do you guys know where The Ruler taught before Saguaro?"

"Beats me," Josh says. "She was already there when I started seventh."

I turn around in my seat.

Junie's gazing at Nerdy Nick, like he's got the answers to all the questions in the universe. Which is bizarro because Junie's mostly the one with the answers.

Sure enough, Nerdy Nick says in his deep, rumbly, full-of-authority voice, "The Ruler came from another Phoenix middle school. Buren Middle School. She had big problems there. Including a dead principal."

chapter
twenty-three

I get home. The Ruler's all mopey, plumping up pillows in the living room, but without her usual enthusiasm for this activity. She's wandering around, muttering about the Saguaro bot's poor performance. "Could you believe it, Sherry? The way the Donner robot kept moving our rings? They earned a lot of extra points from that. And what about when our robot simply stopped? As if the battery were dead." She flops down on the couch. "But it was fully charged."

More and more, I'm believing the stalker played a part in all this robotics stuff. Why? I don't know. Yet. But, for a ghost who can wield a knife, a plastic ring is a walk in the park.

Next, The Ruler does something that I've never

ever seen her do before. Something that tells me she's truly down and depressed. The Ruler slouches. Shoulders rounded over, back humped up. The whole nine yards. And because she's dressed in a beige blouse and a beige skirt and slouching on a beige couch, she kind of fades away.

Ack. Eek. Ike. It's making me sad to see her so sad and beige.

"Have you talked to Dad today?" I ask. That's a conversation that'll usually perk her up like a shot of espresso.

"Yes." And she slouches a little more.

I'm getting desperate here. "And it's your birthday tomorrow. That's exciting."

She gives a beige shrug. "We're celebrating next week when your father gets home."

I clap. "I don't think so."

She startles and sits up a little straighter.

"Your *first* birthday celebration will be tomorrow," I say. "The *second* will be next week."

"Good idea, Sherry," she says slowly. "And I think I'd like my favorite carrot cake with cream cheese icing." She stands. "It's never too early to peel carrots." She marches to the kitchen, her back straight as a, uh, ruler. Yes, she's definitely back.

I head for the privacy of my room. I haven't visited my fish all day, and I'm majorly missing them. Which means they're majorly missing me.

Cindy and Prince are zipping around without a care in the world, which is the way it should be if you're a bala shark. I stuff the fish food in my backpack. I'll carry it with me everywhere so the stalker can't get his ghostly hands on it. He is so not overfeeding my precious adorable fish. Polly was right again; I do have to watch out for them.

Cross-legged on the floor by the aquarium, I text Junie.

`<the stkr is a GHOST!!>`

I wait. My phone sits like a lump of The Ruler's hot oatmeal cereal.

Cindy's cute tail gleams and glints as she flips it against a plastic plant.

I wait some more. More lumpish behavior from my phone.

Prince opens and closes his little mouth against the glass.

I text again.

`<lets go 2 buren aftr last period 2morro. we'll b fake reporters 4 school paper.>`

I wait. And wait. And wait.

I text her again.

`<where r u?>`

Radio silence.

What's the scoop with Junie?

Eventually, I give up and go to bed. Sleeping is a special talent of mine. Homework not done? Big test the next day? Übermessy room? I still sleep great.

So I am majorly peeved when it's five in the morning and I've barely dozed. Even the soothing buzz of the aquarium pump isn't hypnotizing me back to sleep.

I'm lying in bed, grumpy at the world, when I hear a noise. A trucky noise. It rattles and groans and brakes right outside our house.

I swing my legs over the side of the bed and stumble to the window. With my fingers, I tweeze apart the blinds and stare out.

A rusty, dented truck is squished right up against the curb. The driver door opens, then shuts. A guy in a baggy T-shirt with a huge peace sign, faded jeans and sandals is ambling up our walkway with a bouquet of flowers. The same kind of bouquet I didn't get from Josh.

I zoom downstairs to the front-door peephole. And just as he's laying the bouquet on the porch, I whip open the door. "Who are you?"

He jumps back, practically to the other side of the street. His jaw flaps open and shut. A little like my fish, but nowhere near as cute.

I repeat, "Who are you?"

From behind me, I hear the squish-squish of The Ruler's sensible crepe-soled shoes. I'd forgotten how ridiculously early she gets up.

"Who are you?" I say again.

The Ruler lays a hand on my shoulder. "Sherry, he's my ex-husband."

chapter
twenty-four

The Ruler has an ex-husband!

The world has obviously gone wacko. Next thing I know, they'll be serving chocolate burgers and red licorice fries for lunch at the school cafeteria.

The Ruler explained everything. Including how the flowers I originally thought were from Josh were actually from her hippie ex-husband and for her.

Despite my reeling brain and extreme exhaustion, I drag myself to school. No one even notices the dark circles under my eyes. Not one friend. Not one teacher. Not one custodian.

Junie texts me back right before first period. Finally. Zippity-quick we plan two sleuthing field trips for after school. At this time, I will have a friendly-but-firm chat with her about the importance of returning texts in a timely fashion + successful detecting.

I don't see Josh at lunch because it's pizza day for the team on the pool deck. I don't see Junie at lunch because it's pizza day for the robotics team in The Ruler's math room. I sit with my sandwiches in the lunch area across from boy-crazy Brianna, who basically babbles for the entire forty minutes. I yawn five times.

Then I yawn my way through my afternoon classes. Finally, after what feels like foreverland, the longest last period in Saguaro Middle School history comes to a boring end. Junie and I meet by the giant saguaro statue and hightail it to the bus stop.

"Junie, *so* much junk has happened since yesterday." Luckily, I can walk and talk and suck back sour Gummi Worms all at the same time. I fill her in on the meanness of the stalker and the mysterious silver-box business.

By the time I'm done reporting, Junie's eyes are big and round like large pizzas.

"That's not all." I pick out an orange Gummi Worm. "The Ruler has an ex-husband. He's a hippie with a ponytail who really takes flower power to a whole new level." And I tell her about his crazy flower deliveries. And how he and The Ruler got married super young, but it didn't work out. "Last week's bouquet was for their anniversary. This morning he brought her birthday bouquet."

Now Junie's eyes are the size of extra-large pizzas. Which calls attention to her eyeliner. That she's wearing for the first time ever in her life.

I'll get Josh to find out how Eric feels about Junie.

"What does your dad think?" Junie asks.

"He probably doesn't like it. Although the flowers aren't really personal. The hippie gives them to all sorts of people in his life. It's his way of spreading love and peace in the world." I make a peace sign with my fingers. "The Ruler was planning to tell him to stop. But he said today that he's moving to a commune in Northern California with his girlfriend"— I nibble—"and won't be able to keep up with the flower thing when he's out of state 'cause it'd be too expensive."

Junie reaches for the bag of Gummis.

"Why didn't The Ruler tell you the anniversary flowers were really for her?" Junie says.

"She was embarrassed because I didn't even know she had an ex." The bus arrives and we climb on. "And then it got all messed up because I thought they were from Josh. Plus I'd taken the card."

"You get involved with the weirdest things, Sherry." Junie shakes her head.

"No kidding." I choose a yellow worm.

"Your mom really thinks an amethyst will protect us?" Junie says. "Because this guy sounds like a jerk."

"Tell me about it." I point to the scratches on my legs from the tumbleweed. "I'm just hoping I don't scar."

"The amethyst?" Junie prompts.

"Yeah, yeah, she thinks it'll work." I wave a Gummi. "Those necklaces you saw at Brittani's Baubles were on sale, right?" It's not easy being a detective on a mini allowance.

Junie nods. "I hope they still have some." She pulls out a blue and green worm, her fave.

When we're in our seats, I say, "By the way, what's the deal with not getting back to me last night?"

Junie's face closes up like a sea anemone. "Nothing."

"Excuse me? I send you a text saying the stalker is a ghost, and you don't even respond till this morning? Not even a text back accusing me of being nutzoid?"

"Fine." Junie hmpfs. "My parents took my phone away for the evening."

Well, just toss me out the bus window and run me over. I cannot even remember the last time Junie got in trouble.

"I went over my text limit," she says.

"With who? Your cell plan has more texts than mine."

Junie does this cartoony shifty-eyed look.

It's like sometimes when you're watching a suspense

movie and, all of a sudden, it's clear as a cloudless Arizona sky just who the bad guy is. Well, I suddenly know who Junie's texting. "Nerdy Nick? There's that much robotics junk to text about?"

"You think everyone with Bs, As and a haircut is nerdy." Junie's eyes flash with anger.

I have no answer to that because, well, that is pretty much the universally accepted definition of "nerd." At Saguaro Middle School, anyway. But because I so don't like my best friend to be mad at me, I say, "You obviously know him better than I do. From robotics and all. If you tell me he's not a nerd, I believe it."

"Really, Sherry?" Junie's eyes flash again, but with excitement this time. "He's actually a nice guy. Knowledgeable, helpful, smart."

And there you have it: he *is* nerdy. "Don't forget mean. He makes mega mean comments to me."

Junie crosses her arms. "I'd say the mean comments are mutual."

I twirl a few strands of hair around my index finger, mulling this over. "You might be right."

Junie smiles. "Try being nicer to him. You'll see how he grows on you."

Like fungus. I bite my tongue before the words escape. "Have you thought about pursuing Eric?"

"Uh, no, he's still not my type."

"But, Junie, we'd have so much fun double-dating."

"Not. My. Type."

Fine. I can take a hint.

The bus rumbles to a stop, and we hop down and head across the mall parking lot. At the entrance, I yank on the chrome door handle. Then, arm in arm, Junie and I traipse down the hall, past our usual stops, like Video World and Corndogs R Us and Sequins.

We march into Brittani's Baubles. Two teens with a mission. A mission to stay safe from an evil ghost. Fashionably.

Brittani's is all narrow aisles and stuff dangling off hooks every which way. As in not the roomiest, most organized accessory store you'll ever shop in. But it does have good prices. Junie and I beeline to the sale wall and start pawing through the necklaces.

"I found one!" Junie holds up a dainty silver chain with a purple stone the size of a walnut. Frowning, she bounces the necklace in her palm. "It's tackier than I remembered."

"Tacky?" Junie does not know her gemstones. I twirl the chain in the air, letting the amethyst spin. "See how it sparkles and shines? That's the sign of classy costume jewelry."

"Do you really think The Ruler will wear it?" Junie doesn't sound convinced.

"If I gave The Ruler a stone from the school parking lot taped to a piece of string, she'd wear it," I say.

"So something this cute? Of course she'll wear it. Every day of the week."

We poke through the bazillion necklaces hanging from the bazillion hooks. And manage to scrounge up two more. One for Junie, one for The Ruler, one for me.

At the cash register, I hand the girl my money and make sure she stamps my Brittani's Baubles frequent shopper card. Only one more purchase to go till I get a free bracelet. It pays to shop cheap.

We slip on our necklaces and march back to the bus stop. On to our second field trip. The dangerous one.

chapter
twenty-five

Buren Middle School. Where The Ruler used to teach. Where she had problems. Where a principal died.

After about a fifteen-minute ride, Junie and I exit the bus and gaze around, getting our bearings. First time either one of us has been to Buren. They don't have a robotics team. Or a pool.

"Should we start at the skateboard park?" Junie points across the street.

I nod. Because skateboard parks are always a hotbed of gossip. Seriously. If you're, like, in France or somewhere foreign and you need the scoop on a middle grader, go immediately to the nearest skate park.

We walk over and peer through the chain-link fence.

Two guys are in there, totally decked out in padding and helmets. One has a white helmet with black skulls and crimson eyes. Very fake-o tough. The other guy's helmet is solid blue. Very Wal-Mart.

They're really into their boards, flipping and turning and riding the rail. Impressive moves.

These are fanatical skateboarders who probably have lousy grades and a reputation for ditching class a bunch and only wearing name-brand skate clothes. We have them at my school too. I've heard they don't make reliable boyfriends.

Probably seconds before major dehydration sets in, they break for water.

"Junie, this is our chance." We race around to the gate. Once inside, I call out, "Hi, guys. That's some seriously cool skating you've got going."

"Yeah, duuude," Skull Helmet says.

"Yeah, duuude," Blue Helmet echoes.

If that's the extent of their chattiness, getting info from them is going to be like finding happy students at school during standardized testing week.

"We're doing an article on middle-school principals," Junie says.

"And their skateboarding students." I ad-lib that in at the last minute.

"Past and present principals," Junie adds.

"Are ya gonna take pictures of us in our skate gear?" Skull Helmet asks.

Blue Helmet adjusts his knee and elbow pads.

"Natch." I pull out my cell phone.

They both smile like baboons.

"Awesome." I snap a photo. "Who was the last principal at your school?"

"Mr. Haggarty, dude," Skull Helmet says. "He died around the same time my big brother graduated. So, like, a couple of years ago."

Chu-chu-ching! Pay dirt! Someone with a connection to the story.

"Does the name 'Ms. Paulson' ring a bell with you?" Junie asks.

"Skinny math teacher with posture? Crazy wanted to start a robotics club here?" Skull Helmet says. "Yeah, her name rings a bell. She was my brother's teacher. My mom loved her. Even had her over to the house for dinner a few times."

Chu-chu-ching! More pay dirt! "But wait, you don't have a robotics club," I say.

"Jerky Mr. Haggarty wouldn't go for it," Skull Helmet says.

Blue Helmet's bobbing his head, his mouth slightly open. I wonder if maybe he only recently started wearing a helmet. Like after severely knocking his noggin on a skate ramp.

"Was there animosity between Ms. Paulson and the principal?" Junie asks, pulling out a notebook and fake-reportering it.

"Ani-what?" Skull Helmet twirls the wheels on his board. "Like Japanese cartoons?"

Blue Helmet stops bobbing his head. "Ms. Paulson and Mr. Haggarty were, like, total friction."

He speaks. I witnessed a miracle at the park.

"Yeah, dude, that's so true," Skull Helmet says. "But the parents loved Ms. Paulson. They were, like, majorly bummed when she left. The PTA got a gazillion signatures on a petition to get her back and get rid of him."

"No way," I say. This could seriously annoy a principal.

"Yes, way," Skull Helmet says. "My mom still says Ms. Paulson was the only middle-school teacher who could actually teach math. And how that idiot Mr. Haggarty chased her off."

"How'd he die?" Junie asks.

"Was Ms. Paulson involved?" I ask.

Skull Helmet looks at me like I just said something totally off the wall. Along the lines of, do you eat five servings of fruits and veggies every day? "Heart attack. In his office after school."

"Ya wanna hear about the principal we have now?" Skull Helmet asks.

"Maybe some other time," I say.

I barely get the sentence out, before both guys throw down their boards and take a running jump at them.

The gate creaks open behind us. "Hi, Junie. Hi, Sherry."

I spin around.

Nerdy Nick!

He strides toward us, hands in his pants pockets. "How's the article for the school paper going?"

Only one other person in the whole entire world knew of my brilliant plan to pose as school reporters doing a story on Buren. And that one person is blushing the deepest, darkest red any middle schooler has ever blushed.

But what is Nerdy Nick doing here? Why would he take time from his busy study schedule for a fake-o interview at Buren?

And then I know. And then I'm annoyed. At Junie. And at myself.

Have I been living under a rock?

chapter
twenty-six

With bent elbows and tight fists, I'm speedwalking outta that skate park. I'd run, but my feet haven't totally healed from my trek across the desert.

Junie's scrambling behind me. "Sherry"—she huffs like a breaking-down DustBuster—"I'm sorry. I'm really sorry."

"Yeah, well, there are secrets you don't keep from your best friend!" I yell over my shoulder because she's so far behind. "Even if she should figure them out herself because she's a detective. You should be up-front and tell her. Sharing about boyfriends is an important part of teen friendship." I get to the bus stop way before her and stand there, arms crossed, fuming.

Eventually, Junie arrives, all splotchy-faced.

I turn my back. "Where is Nick, anyway?"

"His mom's picking him up." She sucks in a few noisy breaths. "Look, Sherry—"

"Why didn't you just tell me about you two?" I face Junie.

"I wasn't sure how to tell you"—she pushes hair off her sweaty forehead—"without it ending up in a big, messy scene like this."

I cross my arms tighter.

"You're going to get over this, Sherry," Junie says, "so we can double-date."

Zing.

She got me on my weak spot. Because I've been dying to double-date for years and years. Ever since I played Barbies.

"And it's not like he's in on the mystery or anything. He thinks we went to Buren so you could learn more about The Ruler now that she's in your family." Junie holds up her fingers in the sign of a promise. "I'll never ever tell him about your mom and the Academy."

I uncross my arms.

"And I'm not a romance expert like you. I'll need lots of advice," Junie continues.

When she puts it that way, I can see how it's pretty much my duty as a BFF to accept Nick as Junie's squeeze. "Fine, fine. Let's hit Drinks & Stuff, split a strawberry smoothie and get down to the nitty-gritty about guys."

We hug, then clamber on yet another bus. While it's chugging along, we figure out the next step in identifying the stalker. A step that involves Amber.

Back at the mall, we're off to the makeup section at the department store. Amber's working the first counter. Standing next to a woman with blue hair, she's mixing a couple of colors of eye shadow together. She's your basic beauty genius.

"Amber," Junie says. "Can I order you something from Drinks and Stuff?"

Amber looks up. "The usual. My break's in ten minutes."

Drinks & Stuff is in the food court and sells, well, drinks and snacky and sandwichy stuff. Junie and I order, then plunk down on swivel chairs.

"So, Junie." I lean over the table and slurp some of our smoothie. "Let's talk boyfriend business."

She sticks her straw in our cup. "Give me the scoop on kissing."

"Whoa there, missy. Let's not get ahead of ourselves." How can someone who does quadratic equations in her sleep not know about breaking things down into little steps? Because there is an order to romance. I start prying. "Have you guys held hands?"

"Yes." Junie sips. "I like holding hands with Nick."

"Really? 'Cause his hands look kind of dry."

Junie rolls her eyes. "Nick's hands are not dry. The hand holding is way cool."

I'm nodding like a guidance counselor. "Yeah, I get where you're coming from. I'd be blissfully happy if I did nothing all day except hold hands with Josh." I consider the logistics of this for a sec. "Well, except when I'm hungry. For some foods, like a double burger, you just need two hands or it's messy."

Junie looks kind of surprised, like she hasn't thought this through. Then she nods. "Gotcha."

"How about hugging? Done that yet?"

Lips turned down, Junie says, "Almost, but we had bad timing. Our arms were out, then my parents walked in."

"Hugging is so sick," I say. "It's like the 3-D *Star Wars* puzzle you have. Where everything just fits together. Of course, there's also the warmth factor. All that body heat."

"I can't wait." With her straw, Junie stirs swirls in our smoothie.

Only I'm not sure it'll be such an excellent experience for Junie. Nick is basically bony with a caved-in chest.

"How tough is it to get the kissing right?" Junie leans forward, not wanting to miss even one syllable of my important message.

I give a little secret smile. I remember back when I

worried about such stuff. "With the right person, like Josh is for me, kissing just happens perfectly. No teeth crashing. No cut lips. No bad-breath issues." I don't say it, but I can't imagine things will go so easily for Nick and Junie.

"What's it like?" If she leans any closer to me, her amethyst will dip into our drink.

"It's like all the things you, Junie Carter of Phoenix, Arizona, love: ice cream with sprinkles, quadratic equations, Latin club, dumb practical jokes. It's those things all rolled together in a big rubber-band ball that's bouncing around inside you with each kiss. And even when the kiss is over, the ball is still bouncing. Maybe for minutes. Maybe for hours."

"Wow." Junie's got the same look on her face she gets when she's gaping around the computer store at the mall.

"Hey, kiddos." Amber sashays into Drinks & Stuff. Every guy stares.

She poufs up her shoulder-length blond hair. "Where's my latte?"

I push back my chair. "It's probably ready." Junie's better at talking Amber into stuff.

I grab her coffee, a straw and a java jacket. Amber has sensitive fingers. I hang back, holding on to her order, while she and Junie discuss. Amber pulls out her cell and texts. More discussion.

After several minutes, Junie gives me the nod to let

me know they've finished with business. I meander over.

Amber reaches for the cup. "Thanks. Light on the whipped, right?"

"Yuppers." I know the drill.

"Cool." She flashes me a pearly white smile.

"Amber, any tips on making my lips thicker?" I ask.

She regards me, one emerald eye closed. "There's this new lip liner from Paris. Pricey, but it has a plumping factor."

As she's walking away, her hips swaying like a hula hoop, she turns and says, "Not that you really need it, Sherry. Your lips are good."

I can't hold back a full-lipped grin. Then, I say to Junie, "So?"

"Ghost hunting. Tonight. Late. And Zane even said he'd bring his brand-new gaussmeter."

chapter
twenty-seven

It's dusk. The Ruler's in the kitchen whipping up a special organic birthday dinner, involving cabbage casserole. Sam's in the office, zoned out on the computer.

In other words, they're both überoccupied with activities they love and that will keep them busy and away from me. I zip outside to the pear tree and start waving around espresso beans.

I'm thinking Mom thoughts and windmilling my arms like I'm a little Dutch girl when suddenly it smells like the coffee aisle at the grocery store. My branch rattles. Grandpa glides in on Mom's java breeze and lands next to me.

He beak-pokes at my pocket. I pull out a few

sunflower seeds mixed with dust and lint, and he settles in for some palm pecking.

"Hi, Sherry," Mom says. "Lots to catch up on."

"Seriously," I say, then spill about the meanie dead principal who didn't get along with The Ruler. "He could easily be a ghost with an agenda. Tonight, we're going with Zane, Amber's new, ghost-hunting boyfriend, back to Buren to see if the principal's there. Zane says unhappy ghosts usually hang out where they died."

"True," she says.

"Can you watch The Ruler tonight? No way you're going to Buren with all that ghost-hunting equipment. Right, Mom?" I shiver at the memory of the psychic fair when the meter tracked her.

"Right." The branch shakes; she's probably shuddering at the thought too. "And I see you've got a new necklace." The stone sways as Mom checks it out. "That's quite the amethyst. You couldn't find anything less gaudy?"

Gaudy? Am I the only person in Phoenix with a sense of jewelry fashion? "It's gorgeous, Mom. And, before you ask, yes, The Ruler will wear it."

"Wilhelm, can you take tonight's shift?" Mom asks. "I want to finish up the 'About Ghosts Who Don't Move On' tutorial."

Grandpa croaks out a yes.

"The tutorial." I slap my forehead. "Did you learn a bunch?"

"I did." And she pauses. Really pauses. Which means totally bad news for me. "Uh, Sherry . . . the silver box is very light and about the size of a box of Band-Aids. I'm glad about that. I was worried it would be big and heavy."

Grandpa squawks, "It's here," and flies to the knothole above my head.

"I guess Mrs. Howard delivered it earlier today," Mom says.

My eyes are glued to Grandpa's jiggling tail feathers; the rest of him is inside the knothole. Then he completely disappears into the trunk. He's squawking and cawing, all echoey.

I'm about to see and touch a powerful magic box, built for imprisoning an evil ghost. Yikes.

Finally, Grandpa scoots out backward, his yellow feet dangling, his wings bent and crooked. In his beak, he's grasping a slim dull-metal rectangular box.

I pick it up carefully. One side is kind of smushed in. As I turn it over in my palm, it begins to glimmer and gleam, like someone's polishing it. And it's warming up, the way Play-Doh does when you squeeze it.

My index finger traces the curlicue pattern that squiggles over both sides. The box isn't completely flat, but slightly curved across the middle.

And the strange thing is, I feel good and comfortable touching it. I've never seen the silver box before, but it somehow feels familiar and friendly, like an old stuffed animal from my childhood.

"Look, Wilhelm," Mom whispers. "The box is shining."

Grandpa hops up my leg and onto my shoulder.

It is shining more and more, almost looking brand-new. "I can't find a latch anywhere. How do you open it?"

"You don't," Mom whispers again. "It opens itself when the time comes."

A tremor snakes up my spine. "You mean, you just sort of wave the box around the stalker and it sucks him in?"

"No," Mom says super slowly. "There are several conditions. First, it must happen at midnight. Second, in a cemetery. Third, and this is the one I don't understand, the ghost and the Keeper of the Box and the box meet and somehow a connection is forged among all three. The Keeper reaches an understanding of why the ghost won't move on. Then he or she helps the ghost reach an understanding of why it's time to move on. At this exact instant, the box opens, and the ghost, willingly, flies in."

My mom doesn't get it. But on a deep gut level, it feels right to me. The box lifts half an inch off my palm and just hovers there.

Grandpa's little beady eyes ogle the box's movement. "Mrs. Howard."

"She was right about Sherry," Mom says in a hushed voice.

I tune them both out. I'm totally focused on the box, which is humming faintly, high-pitched like an all-boys church choir. It's as though a strong invisible fishing line links me with the box, and it's reeling me in ever so slowly and gently, letting me know that I'm the one.

I'm the one it'll team up with.

I'm the one it'll work with.

We're lopsided right now, with only two out of the three of us present.

But when the ghost-stalker arrives, my role will be Keeper of the Box.

chapter
twenty-eight

Mom and Grandpa leave. I slide the box in my pocket,
where it fits perfectly like it's meant to be there.

Ack. Eek. Ike.

I so do not want that responsibility. I so do not want
to talk a scary, mean ghost-stalker into a box. It should
be my mother's job. Or even Grandpa's. Ghosts should
take care of their own problems. Not be dragging innocent teenagers into their business.

I'm getting ready to climb down when the back
door opens. It's The Ruler. She's wearing her gardening apron with the big pockets. She's toting her little
gardening kneeling pad and her little bucket of tools
and plant vitamins.

Hidden by leaves, I watch, my eyes all squinty to

make out what she's doing. She drops her foam kneeling pad on the grass and sets the bucket next to it. She takes a spray bottle from one of the front apron pockets and drenches her precious tomato plants. I don't even need to be close to recognize the bottle's contents: dish soap and water. The Ruler's method for encouraging pests to leave her tomatoes alone. She won't use insecticide because she's all about nature and being natural.

After pushing the bottle back in her pocket, she pulls out a little mesh bag full of ladybugs. The Ruler uses them in her garden to munch the bad bugs. Strange thing about ladybugs, they don't fly too far from home.

A smell of honey + dirty socks breezes by me.

I stiffen.

The Ruler unties the mesh bag and starts gently tipping ladybugs onto the tallest tomato plant. Suddenly, the bag is ripped from her hand. Hanging upside down above her head, it shakes violently. Ladybugs topple out. The empty mesh bag plops to the ground.

A wave of wind whooshes through our backyard, scattering the ladybugs.

The Ruler is still on her knees, her mouth open.

Finally, I get it together and jump down from the tree. Yanking off my necklace, I swing it wildly above my head.

The air clears and goes back to smelling like, well, like our backyard. The ladybugs are all long gone, up and over our fence, away from the friendly tomato plants.

I reach out a hand to The Ruler, who's looking pretty dazed. I pull her to her feet and into a hug. I don't hug her much, but I think she really needs it today. We both do.

"Okay, that was a weird wind," I say, stepping back. "Good thing ladybugs are so cheap."

"I think I'll brew a cup of chamomile tea." She picks up her kneeling pad.

Before grabbing the bucket, I push the necklace into my pocket. Arm in arm, the two of us trudge to the porch, where we dump the gardening things, then head into the kitchen.

I immediately plug my nose. Cabbage. Smells. Bad. Very. Bad.

"I need something stronger than tea," The Ruler announces, her face all scrunched up, thinking. "Liquid vitamins."

While she's marching from cupboard to cupboard, snapping up junk like the blender and mysterious bags of powder and nonfat plain yogurt, I mess with my amethyst necklace. The clasp is bent from where I yanked it off, but I manage to get it to stay closed.

"Paula! Sherry!" Sam shouts from the office. "You gotta see this!"

We hurtle down the hall. Sam's leaning back in the office chair, pointing to the computer screen. "You will not believe this YouTube." He clicks on the arrow to play.

Gladiator music blares from our computer speakers. The camera zeroes in on a robot. It's Donner's bot. Close shot. Makes the robot look strong and superior. The camera shifts to another robot. Saguaro's bot. It's crying. "Don't make me fight. I'm too wimpy. And I'm not put together right," the bot whines.

Big masculine drums thumping in the background, Donner's robot totally annihilates ours. Until it's a puddle of parts. Then their robot, a victory fist in the air, stands on ours.

It's when I see the last frame of the video that another piece of the mystery falls into place.

chapter
twenty-nine

"I know what plan B is!" I say to Junie on the phone. "Check out this YouTube." I tell her the URL.

I'm in my room, hanging with my fish, waiting while Junie checks out the video.

"So a violent video of their robot beating up our robot was plan B?" she says.

"Pretty lame-o, isn't it?" I say.

"Kind of," Junie says, "but it's kind of smart too. It gets them in this winner mind-set. Which they need after we whomped them so badly last year. And freaking us out only helps their cause. I bet they were planning to make sure we saw it before an actual competition."

"Ya don't think plan B could've been more

substantial?" Cindy flits to the side of the tank and gapes at me.

"You know, Sherry, there's a lot more to robotics than just robotics. There's major mind games too."

"Uh-huh." Sometimes you just gotta let Junie drone. Cindy opens her mouth again. "Tonight's a go, right?"

"Absolutely. Be on your curb at ten. Bring a flashlight and an open mind. Orders from Zane via Amber."

"You wanna sleep over?" I ask. "We can sneak in and out together."

"Sounds good." Junie checks with her mom, who gives her the parental okay because tomorrow is Professional Development Day for teachers and there's no school.

My phone beeps. "Gotta go, it's Josh." I click over.

"Hi, Sherry," he says. "What're ya doing tonight? Coach just canceled the six a.m. polo practice."

Rats. We cannot seem to get on the same schedule.

"I've got a couple of Blockbuster coupons. We could stay up late and watch movies. I'd even go for a chick flick."

Double rats. "Um . . ."

"My mom said she'd buy us candy."

That clinches it. There's only so much temptation a girl can take. "How about one movie and a really spooky adventure?" I tell him about the ghost hunting and Junie spending the night.

I've barely clicked my cell shut when Sam wheelies into my room. "Dinner."

"Uh, Sam. Out! You know you're not allowed in here."

He walks over to my aquarium and gazes in. "So, Josh is coming over?"

He was eavesdropping. How much did the little twerp hear? "Maybe."

"And you guys are going ghost hunting?"

Yikeserama!

"Listen," I say. "You can play some video games with us if you don't tell."

His face is all wrinkled with worry. "Sherry, what if a ghost gets you?"

My breath catches. I have the same fear. "A ghost isn't going to get me," I make myself say. "It's all, like, for fun." Then I choke out, "Who believes in ghosts anyway?"

He lurches across the room and wraps himself around my legs. "I do. I saw a show about them on the Discovery Channel."

"You can't believe everything you see on the Discovery Channel, Sam."

He looks at me like I said you can't believe everything Einstein said. "It was the Discovery Channel, not the Disney Channel."

"Fine. I'll be careful," I say. "Übercareful."

"Pinky promise?"

I poke out my baby finger and we hook together. My brother's basically creeping me out. I mean, I've been pushing my nervousness about tonight into a cobwebby corner of my mind. He's shining a flashlight on it.

"Why don't I come too?" Sam asks.

"Because you're eight. It's for older kids." I'm almost happy when The Ruler calls for us to hurry downstairs. Cabbage casserole might be less painful than this conversation.

I'm pleasantly surprised at the dinner table. If you can get past the fumes, cabbage casserole is a dish of deliciousness. Cheesy sauce with a hint of walnuts and tofu that melts in your mouth. Sam and I both wolf down our portions.

"I think I better make that recipe again," The Ruler says with a proud smile.

"Yeah, like tomorrow night." I grin.

Sam just grunts, his mouth full.

Dessert is also heavenly. Moist carrot cake with honey-sweetened cream cheese icing. The Ruler loves to cook for us and she's quite possibly the only person in the world who can make me crave healthy food.

"Here's a present for you." I hand her a gift bag.

"I have one too." From under his chair, Sam hauls out his most recent Scout project. A leather key ring thingie.

The Ruler is smiling so big I'm worried her face will crack. She dangles the key ring in the air. "Sam, this is beautiful. I'll transfer my keys to it tonight." She opens my gift bag. Eyes glistening, she swings the necklace slowly in the air. She points to my necklace. "We'll be matching. Oh, Sherry, you don't know how happy this makes me."

Or safe. "Let's make a pact. Every day that I wear it, you wear it, and vice versa."

The doorbell rings. It's Josh with a movie and a big bag of candy. He and Sam mess around on a video game while I clean up the kitchen without complaining—a little extra birthday gift. The Ruler calls my dad, her fingers rubbing the amethyst while she chats. When she's done, she passes me the phone.

"How're you doing, pumpkin?" Dad asks. "No more slashed tires, at least."

"Nah, we're good."

"Grandma called to say she sprinkled burnt cloves all over the house," Dad says. "And something about a special wren. I swear she's getting more eccentric with age."

"Yeah, well, with all that clove stuff, it smells very Christmasy here, Dad. You walk in the front door and you pretty much start singing 'Santa Claus Is Coming to Town.'"

He laughs. "I miss your sense of humor when I'm away, Sherry. I'm sure having you around is helping keep Paula's spirits up. And how thoughtful of you to give her a necklace for her birthday."

All these compliments have me glowing like a night-light. We say our goodbyes and I-love-yous, and it's Sam's turn on the phone.

The Ruler stays in the kitchen on her laptop. Sam eventually moves into the office and onto the computer. Junie shows up and hangs in the living room with Josh and me, watching a fairly dumb movie. Which is fine. Sitting next to Josh, I could watch preschooler programs and still be stoked.

Slowly, slowly the clock ticks until The Ruler and Sam, who both have the same bedtime, come in to tell us goodnight. When no one's looking, he mouths at me, "Be careful."

I give him a thumbs-up.

"You're all set for a ride?" The Ruler asks Josh.

"Yeah, I'm good." He just doesn't say his ride is from Amber and it's to Buren Middle School.

Josh, Junie and I finish the movie. I can barely concentrate on the screen 'cause I start imagining all the things that can go wrong when you're sneaking out of your house at night on a mission to find an evil ghost.

Junie's cell rings. It's Amber. She's here.

chapter
thirty

I slowly twist the knob on the porch door, then creep through. Josh and Junie follow me. I leave the door unlocked so Junie and I can get back in later. We duck under the motion light. I creak open the gate.

We're tiptoeing down the walkway to the curb when we pass Grandpa perched on the porch.

Even with The Ruler wearing the amethyst, he's not taking chances, but standing guard. Anyway, the necklace is probably in her jewelry box for the night. A stone that large could puncture a lung. I sleep with mine under my pillow.

"Good luck," Grandpa squawks.

I give a half-nod. My heart's pounding hard enough to bust out of my rib cage. I so want Mr. Haggarty to be the ghost-stalker. 'Cause once we know the stalker's identity, Mom, Grandpa and I can start figuring out why he won't move on. I'll use all that info to connect with him at the cemetery and convince him to fly into the silver box. Every one of these steps is a step closer to Real Time with Mom. But this nocturnal field trip to Buren is massively scary.

"Call if you need us." Grandpa fixes me with a serious look to let me know he means business and he wants me safe.

"That bird just cawed." Josh frowns. "I thought birds slept at night and got up, like, really early."

"Urban myth," I say, all noncommittal.

"Definitely," Junie agrees.

At the front of the house, I glance up at Sam's bedroom window. Dark. And there's no movement at the blinds. Phew. I so don't need a little brother mixed up in this dangerous business.

I clutch Josh's hand, and we climb into the backseat of Amber's car. Junie's in the front with her cousin. A feeling of relief rushes through me when I realize Nick is absent. Of course, I'll make an enormous effort to get along with him. At some point. Of course, we'll double-date. At some point. But I can't handle being nice tonight, given all the spectral stress.

"You've got flashlights?" Amber says.

"Yeah," I say. It's not that she's worried about us

tripping over a tree root in the dark. No, no, no. She's worried we'll annoy her new, ghost-hunting boyfriend and cramp her style.

You'd think Josh'd be übercurious about this evening. Truth is, he isn't a guy who questions much. More of a go-with-the-flow personality. Which works well given my secret assignments with the Academy.

We arrive at Buren, and Zane's van is already in the parking lot, under a bright light. How do I know it's his? First off, no one else is here. Second, spray painted in Day-Glo orange on the side, it says, THE GHOST HUNTER, ZANE BROWN. CALL FOR ANY AND ALL PARANORMAL CONCERNS. Then there's a phone number. Third, the hatch is up, and he's hauling out junk and piling it on the sidewalk.

Amber squeals in next to the van. The engine's barely off before she's out and hanging on Zane.

The rest of us exit and join them on the sidewalk. I'm sniffing up a storm. No honey + dirty socks. Not yet, anyway.

"This is Josh Morton," I say, "my boyfriend." I still get a flutter in my stomach every time I say that.

"Hi, dude." Zane's kneeling, sorting through his stuff and trying to keep his balance with Amber all over him. He practices our names in case we get into a sticky situation and he needs to shout out to us. "I'm happy to lead you all. Just remember to do what I say, and nobody'll get hurt." He gazes at us like we're his kindergarten class. "Let me assign everyone a piece of equipment." He closes one eye, like he's truly sizing up our individual supernatural talents.

He does not look at me and say, "Dude, this chick can smell ghosts and talk to them. She's awesome." Instead, he unzips a lumpy backpack and draws out a tape recorder. "You're in charge of audio for EVPs. If you hear any electronic voice phenomena, hit Record."

Yikes.

"What about me?" Junie asks.

"Hmmm." Zane rubs his cute but pointy chin, then hands her a digital camera. "You're watching for light anomalies, ectoplasmic mists, that sort of thing." Next he gives Josh eighteen-inch L-shaped copper rods.

"These are dowsing rods. Hold them out straight in front of you, man," Zane says.

Josh sticks his arms out, zero bend at the elbows. "Then what?"

"If we encounter paranormal activity, the rods will cross, producing an orb. Junie will snap a picture of the orb. Sherry will record any voices or sounds."

"What about me, Zane?" Amber looks at him with big emerald eyes. Which are really brown eyes covered with green contact lenses, but he doesn't know that. He probably also doesn't know about her school boyfriend.

"You can help me with the gaussmeter. And you can

carry the infrared noncontact thermometer. And you can be in charge of the materials in the backpack. And you can carry a flashlight. And you can tell others when to turn their flashlight on or off."

All these "ands" make Amber a happy camper. She does enjoy bossing Junie and me around. She waves the thermometer, which looks like a toy gun.

"We can expect a drop of approximately ten degrees with a paranormal presence," Zane says.

I've never noticed that.

"Flashlights on, people," Amber cracks in a drill-sergeant voice. She pokes the thermometer into her jeans pocket.

We head onto campus, armed with our ghost-hunting equipment. Junie and I also have our amethyst necklaces. And I have my nose.

It's dark, but not pitch black because the school's shining some powerful lights that apparently stay on all night. Plus, we've been ordered to use our flashlights.

"Time for some general rules about ghost hunting," Zane says. "Number one: Only go with a professional. Like me. Number two: Scope out the haunting location during daylight. I investigated the location this afternoon. Number three: Have the proper ghost-hunting equipment. Once again, you guys have me."

Blah blah blah. Got it. You're the expert. But we've also got a mean ghost-stalker with an agenda. And whose name is on the agenda? Not yours. Mine. What am I supposed to do if the stalker comes after me specifically? In front of everyone? And hurts me? Or worse yet, trips me and makes me look like a total dork?

"What if the ghost is mean?" I ask. "How do we protect ourselves?"

"Good question, Sherry." Zane stops walking, shrugs off his backpack and starts rooting around in it.

Amber rolls her eyes at me.

Zane hands each of us a small plastic bag with about a half a cup of something herbalish. "Open the bag if you're in danger and let the spirits get a whiff. It's cloves."

So not filling me with confidence.

"This really works?" Junie's frowning. "What about an amethyst?"

"I prefer cloves." Zane waves his hand at our necklaces, dismissing the whole amethyst idea. "For a group, cloves are more cost-effective. If things really go south, though, I'll take it to the next level. I have a method where I lure the spirit onto my back. Very fatiguing, but a special piggybacking talent I have."

What is this guy blathering about?

"So what do we do?" Josh asks, all confused.

"If a spirit is bothering you and the bag of cloves doesn't banish him, I'll get down on my hands and knees, right close to you. The spirit will jump on my back, and I'll take control of the situation."

Junie and I raise our eyebrows at each other. Josh shrugs. Not like he really believes in ghosts anyway. Amber takes a baby step away from Zane. She tolerates little to zero weirdness in boyfriends. And Zane is close to crossing the line.

"We'll walk around the school, concentrating especially on the office area." Zane swings his backpack on and we start shuffling along again. "In general, we're on the lookout for footsteps, weird smells, shadows that don't make sense, doors opening and closing, lights switching on and off, sounds. Alert me immediately. I'm the expert."

There's a knot the size of Phoenix + Tucson + Flagstaff in my stomach.

Josh transfers both rods to one hand, then squeezes my shoulder with the other. "You okay, Sherry? You're so quiet."

"I'm okay." If you only knew, dear cute, adorable boyfriend who thinks I'm normal. If you only knew how unokay I am.

Junie frees up a hand by sticking her flashlight under her arm. She squeezes my other shoulder.

How weird is it that even though I'm flanked by two people who really care about me, I feel überalone?

Zane picks up the pace until we're standing in front

of the office door. The one with the sign that says ALL VISITORS MUST REPORT TO THE OFFICE.

"Josh, my man, time to get those copper dowsing rods into position. Junie, Sherry, be at the ready with your equipment." All military, Zane spreads his legs apart. Elbows straight, he holds out the gaussmeter. "I. Am. Now. Turning. On. The. Meter."

Our eyes glued to the thin red needle, we lean toward Zane and his magic machine. Zane thumb-flicks the On switch.

And . . . nothing. Nada. Zilch.

The needle doesn't waver, doesn't quiver, doesn't budge.

Slowly, slowly, we trek around the school. We're dead quiet, totally focused on every sound, every movement, every breath.

My muscles ache with tension. Like the day after we do weights in PE. Josh is mummy-walking, the dowsing rods out in front of him. Junie's index finger hovers above the shutter button. Zane handles his expensive meter like he's in charge of the royal jewels. In one hand, Amber waves the digital thermometer. In the other, she's manning a flashlight, sweeping its arc of light on the ground in front of us so we don't stumble over stray trash.

We search the north side of the school.

Nothing.

The east side.

Nothing.

The west side.

Nothing.

The south side.

Nothing.

Back at the office door, Josh lowers the dowsing rods. The camera whirrs as Junie switches it off. Without discussion, we congregate in a circle. Very horror-movie-ish.

I blow out a breath and begin to relax from the neck down. Vertebrae by vertebrae I'm turning rubbery.

"I'm bored." Amber's whine slices the night air. "Let's go to a club or something, Zane."

Annoyance flits across his face.

With furrowed brow, Zane looks each of us in the eye. He saves Amber for last. "Team, we've done good work here. The area is clean." He clicks off the meter. "I sense some disappointment. And I don't like disappointed troops. Let's move our operation elsewhere. According to a fellow ghost hunter I had lunch with today, there is a middle school in the area with paranormal activity.

"Donner."

chapter
thirty-one

Leaning against the office door at Donner Middle School, Amber announces, "I'm still bored."

Sounds like Zane's already traveling the exit ramp on Amber's freeway of romance.

Zane ignores her. "We need to be extra careful here. Because we've broken rule number two. I did not check out the location during daylight hours."

"I know my way around the pool area," Josh says.

Zane ignores him. The Ghost Hunter is a focused dude.

I don't mention that I know which sidewalk leads to the computer lab, home of the Donner robotics club.

We get all organized. Junie turns on the camera. Josh has the dowsing sticks out and in position. I'm carrying the tape recorder. Amber's scowling and twirling the thermometer in the air. Zane, of course, guards the gaussmeter. Everyone has a flashlight.

Amber stands at attention. "Flashlights," she intones, "on."

Zane goes still, his head at an angle. "There's a buzz in the air here. A paranormal energy. I can feel it."

There's a buzz in my stomach too. Called panic + fear. *Sniff. Sniff.* Everything smells normal.

"So, Zane," I say, "how hard is it to identify a ghost? As in, get their name?"

"Depends on the ghost." He doesn't even look at me; he's dialing into the atmosphere. "A friendly ghost might tell you his name. An unfriendly ghost? You gotta put together the clues, ask questions of the living. It's not easy."

So not the answer I want.

We move en masse toward the pool, like a giant bug with ten legs and ten pairs of eyes. Off-key, Amber's humming a vaguely familiar song.

"You okay?" Junie murmurs to me.

I shrug. "Barely."

"Something's here," Zane whispers. "The hairs on my arms are standing up."

I'm not sure how he can tell with a long-sleeved T-shirt on, but I'm buying it. And edging toward freak-out.

We plod around the pool. A breeze comes up. I'm

sniffing so hard, I'll probably end up with a hugely embarrassing nosebleed.

"Nothing here," Zane says. "Let's head back to the school buildings."

Another breeze. Zane stops. "The needle's moving."

We all crowd around. Sure enough, it's wavering. Faintly. In fact, you could easily miss the movement if you weren't staring with bugged-out eyeballs.

Amber stops humming.

The dowsing rods begin to shake, ever so slightly. "It's not me," Josh says. "I'm trying to hold them still." His arm muscles are taut with effort.

Junie points the camera at the L-shape where the ends of the rods meet.

And then I smell it. Faintly. The telltale scent of honey + dirty socks.

Yikes!

I poke the flashlight in my pocket, then, with my free hand, reach to rub the amethyst.

It's not there!

The clasp! It was warped from when I ripped the necklace off earlier in the garden. The necklace must have slipped off in the car.

Yikes!

Should I run for it? Leave the safety of my friends? And Zane's equipment and his bizarre piggyback technique? Is the necklace for sure in Amber's car?

I rack my brain. Yes! I can definitely remember

touching the amethyst on the ride between the two middle schools.

The stalker smell gets stronger.

"Look at the meter now!" Zane says.

The needle's jumping and jiggling like kids at an after-school dance.

The rods are shaking. Josh is quiet, concentrating, staring at the ends.

I shove my hand in my pocket. "Zane," I say all hysterical, "you didn't give us the cloves."

"Amber," Zane says in a low voice, "reach into my backpack. Very slowly. Don't scare the spirit." His eyes widen. "The meter's really going ballistic!"

Sure enough, the needle's bobbing and peaking and dancing and prancing. My pulse is doing the same thing.

I mouth to Junie, "He's here!" I point to my bare neck, where there should be a protective amethyst necklace.

"Get the cloves now, Sherry," Junie says.

The honey + dirty socks smell is nauseatingly strong.

"That's *my* job." Amber reaches for the zipper. She grabs hold of the tab and pulls. The zipper's teeth yawn open.

The zipper closes. Fast.

Amber frowns, guiding the zipper open again.

The zipper snaps shut.

"Sherry, I don't like cloves," the ghost-stalker says.

"Tell your friend not to waste her time. I could do this all night."

I open my mouth to scream, but nothing comes out.

The dowsing rods start shaking and jerking like they're in seizure mode.

"I can barely hold on to these," Josh says through clenched teeth.

Amber reads the thermometer. "Fifty-five degrees."

"That's a drop of ten degrees," Junie says.

An orb glows sickly green between the ends of the two rods. It grows and grows until it's the size of a bowling ball. Shimmering and glowing in the night.

Click, click, click. Junie's finger taps on the camera's release button.

The wind roars in my ears. My pulse roars in my ears. I can't tell what's from the ghost and what's from my fright.

The camera is ripped from Junie's hand. Tiny and dark, it sails high above us toward the bright of a school light. With a crash, it smashes into the light and the bulb winks out.

The wind blows strong and noisy. Like the ghost's swirling around us. The rods dance out of Josh's hands and clatter away.

The five of us stand there, silent and stunned.

Junie makes the first move. She unhooks her necklace and whirls it in the air, cowgirl-lasso style.

"This spirit is out of control!" Zane shouts. "I don't think one amethyst will make a difference."

But the wind dies down.

From above us, the ghost-stalker says, "This is between us, Sherry. Your friends can go home."

He sounds like he's around my age! I call out, "Who are you?"

Everyone looks at me like I've totally lost it. Of course, they can't hear him. And they don't know how desperately I need his name for the silver box.

"Get Ms. Paulson to quit robotics." The stalker's blurry shape skitters in the night sky.

He ignored my question, but calling The Ruler Ms. Paulson is a clue that he's not from my school.

"I can make things very ugly," he says, gliding closer to me, "if you don't do what I say."

Like at the Party Store when they inflate balloons with helium, I start filling up with fear.

And then the image of a glittering amethyst twirls into my mind. One amethyst, and he's backing off. Two amethysts might chase him away.

"Let's go," I say. I whisper to Junie that my amethyst is in Amber's car.

"Yeah." Josh grabs my hand. "We're outta here."

"No, no!" Zane drops to his hands and knees. "I've got it covered."

I kick at the sole of Zane's shoe. "Get up! Get up!"

He starts mumbling in some strange language, chanting the same string of sounds over and over.

It's definitely not French. Too many vowels.

"Zane," Amber says, "we're leaving."

The four of us sprint to the parking lot. A breeze blows along with us, but high in the air. I can still smell honey + dirty socks. The ghost is following us!

I'm slightly out in front, determined to get my necklace from Amber's car. As quickly as possible.

My fingers grasp the door handle. The ghost swooshes in close to me. He blows angry smelly air all around.

"Junie!" I yell. "Your necklace!"

Out of the corner of my eye, I see a light bobbing closer and closer to our strange scene. It's a bicycle. The rider is pedaling head down, focused on the pathway. Shoulder-length, midnight black hair flows from under one side of her helmet.

It's Claire!

As she pedals under a light, she looks up and sees me. Her face registers complete and total confusion. Then she glances above me.

I follow her gaze. The ghost-stalker's hazy image hovers. He's staring at Claire.

Still gawking up at the ghost, Claire's headed straight for a post—the post with the robotics meeting announcement. Her lips part and she gasps, "Dylan?"

chapter
thirty-two

The air is totally still. The smell of honey + dirty socks has disappeared. The ghost is gone.

We rush over to Claire. She pushes her bike off her chest and sits up.

I kneel. "You okay?"

She rubs her forehead, right next to a smear of dirt. She glares at me. "What are *you* doing here?"

"Long story, but nothing to do with robotics." While I'm answering her, all kinds of mystery pieces are slotting into place. She saw the ghost. She named the ghost. What is the connection between Claire and the stalker? I need to talk with her alone.

I gesture with my arm to Josh, Junie and Amber. "Maybe you should go check on Zane?"

They leave.

"What's up, Claire?" I ask. "How come you're riding your bike in the middle of the night?"

She stands and brushes bits of grass and dirt off her sweatpants. "Get lost, Sherry."

Obviously not a girl known for her manners. "Look, when I snuck into your robotics club meeting, it wasn't to spy on your program," I say.

Claire rubs her forehead again, still missing the dirt.

Voices float through the dark toward us. Josh, Junie, Amber and Zane are approaching the parking lot. I need info from Claire. Fast.

"So did you see anything weird before you crashed into the post?" I'm watching Claire closely.

She swings a leg over her bike. She avoids my eyes. "Nope."

"You did so. We both did," I say. "A blurry outline of a ghost."

She spins a pedal with her foot, then jerks it to a stop. "I'm going home." She mutters under her breath, "Like I can even concentrate now."

"Claire, you saw a ghost."

She's on her bike and getting her balance.

"Who's Dylan, Claire?"

Without even a wave goodbye, she rides off.

Josh, Junie, Amber and Zane show up. We help Zane pack his ghost-hunting stuff. He's strangely

217

quiet, perhaps plotting a return trip with his ghost-hunter buddies. In other words, without us. Which is okeydokey by me. My next meeting with the stalker will be in a cemetery at midnight. Way frightening.

We wave goodbye as he drives into the night.

"Where's your friend on the bike?" Amber asks.

"Gone home," I say. "But she's not really a friend."

"I guess that's why she got Josh's name wrong." Amber unlocks the car doors.

"I've never seen her before." Josh shakes his head.

"I thought maybe she had you mixed up with another polo player." Junie opens the passenger door.

They all think Claire was referring to Josh when she said "Dylan." They don't realize she was talking to the ghost. Only Claire and I saw the ghost-stalker!

When Amber's backing out, Josh says, "You know, I came tonight for laughs. I never believed in ghosts before. But I sure do now."

Amber nods. "And I am so done with all this. That kind of wind is not good for my skin type."

"What about Zane?" Junie asks. "He's not giving up ghosts any time soon."

"I am so done with him too. That guy is not my type."

Can't argue there. Amber's more into guys with motorcycles and reputations for breaking curfew. Not guys who mumble in a foreign language and who'll always rate a ghost higher than her.

We drive in silence. Because we're totally exhausted. And more than a little freaked. I pat the seat until my fist closes around my necklace.

Tomorrow will bring a big whopping powwow with my mom and grandfather.

chapter
thirty-three

The next morning, Wednesday, Junie and I sleep way late. By the time we make it down to the kitchen, The Ruler and Sam have left. There's a note on the counter, next to a plate of lumpy, jaundiced-looking muffins.

I'm at school. Sam is playing next door with Luke. Baked orange juice–cranberry muffins this a.m. Paula xo

"I'm sure Grandpa tailed her to Saguaro." I scrounge in the cupboard for a couple of plates. "The stalker's really getting powerful. I mean, when he was bugging The Ruler in the backyard and I swung the amethyst, he vamoosed. But at Donner, your necklace only weakened him; he still followed us."

"Scary." Junie picks up a muffin and peels the cupcake liner off. She holds it up close, peering at it.

"Surprisingly good," I say. "Sam and I love them."

Junie sniffs the top of the muffin. "I'll try a bite."

I fill the kettle with water for hot chocolate and instant coffee.

Junie and I spend the night at each other's houses so often that we've perfected our breakfast routine. We don't talk too much, just sort of chill in auto mode at first. She dumps the powder in our mugs. I pour in the boiling water. She adds an ice cube to her hot chocolate.

I set the cup of instant coffee out on the porch to call Mom, then join Junie at the counter.

So there we are, in sweats and T-shirts, perched on bar stools. I plop a few mini-marshmallows in my mug and push the bag over to her. "That was pretty frightening last night."

Junie sticks a spoon in her mug and stirs. "Very frightening. I don't get what happened at the end. Why did he suddenly stop? You never even got the car door open to grab your necklace."

"I think he recognized Claire."

Junie freezes, mid-stir, and waits for me to continue.

"He was this hazy outline above us. When Claire approached, he stared right at her." I slurp some hot chocolate. "Claire saw him too, but she won't admit it."

Junie nibbles the muffin, then sets it down. Her

tongue tip pokes out between her teeth, a sign she's thinking hard. "Have you ever seen a ghost before?"

"No. Only Mrs. Howard, when she lets me. I don't think the ghost-stalker realized I could see him. He was totally focused on Claire. And I think it just sort of happened."

"So who's Dylan?" Junie sips her hot chocolate.

"Beats me," I say. "When you loaded Claire's page on the Donner website, did you read it?"

"No." Junie dumps a mountain of marshmallows in her mug. "I was just throwing material up as fast as I could."

"Let's start there," I say. "Maybe she mentions him."

There's a gentle rapping at the back door and a definite smell of coffee coming from that direction. I go to the porch door to tell my mom the coast is clear and that she, Junie and I need to kick it in the office so we can hit the Internet.

While the computer's booting up, Junie and I fill my mom in on plan B and ghost hunting at Buren and Donner.

I click onto Donner's website and open "Getting to Know Claire."

I think I hear a sound in the hall, but when I turn around, there's nobody. This stalker mystery really has me spooked.

"Listen to this!" Junie reads aloud, " 'My family is

me, my mom and my dad. I'm hard-core into robotics. My brother, Dylan, was too. Here's our family photo.' "

I glance at the picture. "It's him. Even the same all sticky-outy Einstein-ish hair."

Then, my fingers are flying over the keys, Googling Dylan Greene. We're crowded around the screen, waiting for the page to load. I choose the first entry. It's from our school district site.

Dylan Greene, a promising eighth-grade student at Donner Middle School, died today on campus, following a bee sting. The insect flew in through an open classroom window. Dylan is survived by his mother, his father and his younger sister. The Donner Middle School Robotics Team is holding a vigil for him tomorrow evening.

Silence while we digest this. We've identified the stalker. Dylan Greene, deceased rival robotics student, has been trying to creep out The Ruler to the point she quits Saguaro's robotics team.

"Totally explains why Claire wigged when I opened the window at the robotics meeting," I say.

"Maybe she's even allergic to bees herself," Mom says.

"Thing is, no matter how much Dylan bugs The Ruler, she won't quit our team," Junie says. "Not with her competitive, persistent personality."

"It would escalate until he hurt her," Mom says.

"Yeah, he would totally have to take her out of commission," I say.

"Cemetery rendezvous," we say in unison.

I look at Junie. "We'll go to Sun Cemetery? So we can ride our bikes?"

"That works," Junie says. "But I don't understand how we get a ghost to meet us there."

I think I hear a sound again, but no, no one, nothing. This mystery is so messing with my nerves.

"The tutorial said you lure the ghost with objects that were a part of his life." Papers on the desk flutter where Mom's settling in.

"Say what?" I can't help it; my eyes are rolling all on their own. "I take objects from his life and haul them out to the cemetery?"

"It's not just the objects," Mom says. "You have to understand what makes Dylan tick. That's all part and parcel of the connection process among the box and the Keeper of the Box and the ghost."

"Who makes up this stuff?" I thump the desk. "No way I can learn"—I draw quotation marks in the air with my fingers—" 'what makes him tick.' "

"Could you talk to Claire about her brother?" Junie asks.

"Yes, because that crazy, wacked-out robotics nutcase who had her friends ditch me in the desert is dying to spend time with me. No doubt she lies awake at night obsessing, 'I just have to become friends with Sherry, who called herself Mary and lied her way through our robotics meeting. Maybe I can invite her out for a burger and open up to her about my dead brother. Oh yeah, and I'd like to give Sherry a bunch of my brother's belongings.'" I bury my head in my hands. "This is so not happening for us, people."

"If Claire saw Dylan, can she see other ghosts too?" Junie asks.

"Haven't got a clue," I mumble into my palms.

"I see where Junie's going and it's a great idea," Mom says. "Take her an amethyst necklace. It's a way to soften her up. Plus, she may really need the protection."

I look up and repeat what Mom said to keep Junie in the loop.

"What's our timeline?" Junie asks.

Ack. Eek. Ike. Trust Junie to zoom straight to the terrifying stuff. "This is our last day," I say. "We'll have to talk Dylan into the silver box at midnight tonight. Otherwise, Mrs. Howard takes over, and it's goodbye to any Real Time."

Less than twelve hours. It lies like a lump of lead in the middle of the room. Twenty-four hours flies by fast, unless you're studying for a science test. In twelve hours, I'll know if I have Real Time. Or if I don't.

Mom clears her throat. "That settles it, then. Sherry, you go visit Claire this afternoon. Tonight, it's a showdown with a ghost at Sun Cemetery."

Junie munches on a muffin. "I'll meet you at the curb with my bike at eleven o'clock."

I hear another faint scurrying sound. I swear we probably have mice with all the healthy, grainy food The Ruler buys.

"I think we can safely leave The Ruler without protection, because Dylan will be at the cemetery," Mom says.

"Can you and Grandpa get there early and hide?" I ask her.

"Yes, although we have to be far enough away that we don't scare Dylan off," Mom says. "He'll be watching for the silver box and probably assumes I'm a Keeper. If he senses our presence, he'll vanish. So to speak."

I translate for Junie, an avocado-sized knot of dread lodged in my stomach. Just how far away is far enough away? Too far to help if Dylan goes berserko, out of control?

"We call your mom with the coffee beans if we get in trouble?" Junie says in a shaky voice. She's probably got an avocado in her stomach too.

"That's the idea," Mom says. "I'm flying over to your school now to relieve Grandpa of his bodyguarding duties. Then he'll handle reconnaissance at Sun Cemetery."

I repeat what she said for Junie.

After my mom takes off, Junie and I dawdle in the office, deciding on our cemetery outfits: jeans, sweatshirts, athletic shoes. We're going for speed and comfort. Then, we actually study. I've got Polly's psychic advice echoing in my head: *You got a science test coming up? You better study.* Junie never takes chances with her grades.

Later, when we're sitting on the curb out front, waiting for Junie's mom to pick her up, I say, "You know what? I've finally got my Real Time plan. Our living room when no one else is home. I'm gonna set it up like we're a mom and daughter getting together, even though I know she can't eat or anything. So I'll play Mom's CDs for music, get vanilla wafer cookies, which we both used to snack on, and wear my Phoenix Police Department T-shirt."

Now, we just have to pull off tonight. Successfully.

chapter
thirty-four

I lean my bike against the stucco wall and push the doorbell at Claire's house. I pat my jeans pocket, where I've stashed the amethyst necklace, and shrug to straighten my backpack.

"Hello." An older version of Claire, pudgier and with brown hair all the same length, answers the door. She's wearing a Curious George apron. "Can I help you?"

"I know Claire from school. Is she around?"

"You're here to see Claire?" Her penciled-on eyebrows jump up in shock.

I'm guessing Claire doesn't get a ton of unexpected visitors.

"Come in. Come in." She steps back to let me pass. "I'm Sandra, her mother. And you are . . . ?"

I step into the delightful, delicious smell of fresh-baked chocolate chip cookies. "My name's Sherry, but I'd kind of like to surprise her, if that's okay."

Sandra nods knowingly. Claire is obviously difficult at home too. "Would you like some cookies and milk?"

Have I fallen into a black-and-white TV? Is this *Leave It to Somebody or Other*? "Sure." I follow her into a small family room with worn rose carpet and smushed-down cushions on a faded blue couch.

Before I even have a chance to get all comfy and cozy, Claire clomps in from the hallway.

She halts mid-clomp, the shoulder-length side of her hair swinging, and glares. "What are you doing here?"

Sandra tugs gently on Claire's arm. "I need you in the kitchen for a second."

The two of them disappear through an entryway.

I take this opportunity to scan the room for family-ish junk I can use to lure Dylan to the cemetery tonight. Right behind the couch, there's a tall, skinny table loaded down with pictures. Looks like they took a family cruise. There's a picture of Sandra, a man who must be the dad, Dylan and Claire standing in a line in front of a cruise ship. They're all looking reasonably happy. Works for me. I unzip my backpack and drop it in.

From the kitchen, I can hear Sandra's low tones, but I can't hear what she's saying.

"I can't stand her," Claire says. She doesn't lower her voice even one iota.

Can't stand me? Ouchie mama. Claire isn't overly worried about hurting my feelings. Luckily, I'm a thick-skinned detective type.

Four steps and I've zipped across the little room and am peering into a curio cabinet. Mr. Greene's bowling trophy. A cutie-pie brass monkey that must be from a collection of Sandra's. Someone's bronzed baby shoe. A couple of soccer trophies. I snatch up the shoe and the trophies. *Clinkety, clink, clink.* Into the backpack they go.

For good measure, I toss in a few Donner Dynamos team buttons and a Popsicle-stick craft.

"You will sit down with her and have some cookies and milk. To make a friend, you have to be a friend." Sandra has given up on the whispering and is talking loud enough that I can hear her.

"Give me a break," Claire says. "Do you wanna know what she did to me?"

"I do not," Sandra says. "If you want me to take you to Electronics City later today, you'll pick up this tray and march back in there and be polite. For ten minutes. Like a normal girl who has girlfriends over after school."

I'm barely seated on the couch, my legs crossed,

with my lumpy, bumpy backpack by my feet when Claire enters. She's carrying a metal tray loaded down with all sorts of treats, not just cookies.

She clatters the tray on the coffee table, then sinks into a chair kitty-corner to me.

I grab a couple of cookies, still warm from the oven. It's been forever since I've had home-baked cookies with refined sugar and real chocolate chips. The Ruler's baking tends toward muffins and bread. My mom rarely baked. I've never had a Sandra.

"Seriously. I want to know what you're doing here," Claire hisses.

I poke up a finger. "One sec." I close my eyes and bite. And chew. And sigh. If it weren't for the whole ghost-stalker mystery thing, I'd think I was in after-school-snack heaven. I open my eyes. Time to shower Claire with gifts in the hopes she'll pass on info about Dylan.

"I brought the bling." From the front pouch of my backpack, I pull out a plastic bag stuffed with glass gemstones and sequins. "Most of the stones and se-quins are turquoise plus sea green. But there are a few black and white of each."

"Why?" Claire crosses her arms. "It's not like you're on our team."

"Because I said I would. And bling is sort of my spe-cialty. And, honestly, I don't care who wins. And I feel really bad about how things turned out."

Arms still crossed, Claire glares at me.

I set the bag on the table next to the tray. "I'm leaving it here. Use it or not, it's up to you." I point to a couple of the larger turquoise + sea green pieces. "These are perfect for the front of your robot. Very eye-catching."

There's silence while Claire stares at the transparent bag. She doesn't make a move to open it or anything.

"How's Austin?"

"Fine." Claire tears her gaze away from the bling and looks at me. "Give him a voltage meter and some driving time, and he's good as new."

That makes me feel better. I pick up a brownie with white frosting for eyes and a turned-down smile. "What's this?"

"A frownie. My mother's specialty."

Cupping my palm under my chin to catch crumbs, I bite in. It's like a party for my taste buds. "Is there chocolate pudding in here?"

Claire nods. She's not friendly, but she's thawing.

I polish off the frownie. Then, from my pocket, I gently tug out the amethyst necklace. "It's for you."

She doesn't reach for it. "Why?"

I hold the necklace up. On the end of the silver chain, the amethyst spins in the air. "Without going into a bunch of mumbo jumbo, you need to wear this."

She still doesn't reach for it.

"Claire, I know you saw Dylan's outline last night. I saw it too."

She shakes her head.

"We've got some sort of strange talent to do with the spirit world," I say softly. "I didn't ask for it. You didn't ask for it. But we have to keep ourselves safe. And this necklace will do that."

"Did you know I'm so advanced in math, I go up to the high school for classes?" she says. "My world is scientific and logical. I don't do ghosts."

"Claire, I hear what you're saying. I'm not into science or math or whatever, but ghosts don't fit easily into my life either." I swing the necklace slowly. "For whatever reason, though, we're stuck with this strange spiritual gift."

She takes the necklace from me. "You won't believe the weird rituals Dylan always did before competitions."

"Like what?" I grab another frownie. Unless Sandra gives me the recipe and I learn to bake, I won't be eating too many more of these delish numbers after today.

"Eat a peanut butter and honey sandwich. He had that bee-allergy thing going, but, boy, he liked honey." Claire unclasps the necklace and then fastens it around her neck. "And he always wore the same socks. Wouldn't let Mom wash them. He got the idea from the basketball team."

That's just gross, but it explains his smell. Not that Josh doesn't have a ritual regarding a certain water polo cap.

Claire sighs, jutting out her perfectly plump lower lip. "You know why I was at school late last night?"

"Why?"

"I knew something was up with our bot. There is no way we should've killed Saguaro so bad at the practice competition. We're not that skilled at flipping rings off pegs, but we got all yours. We're not that fast at maneuvering around the field, but we beat you by a mile." With the palm of her hand, Claire presses the stone to her chest. "Now I get it. It was Dylan. He doesn't trust me to lead the Donner Dynamos to the championships."

"I don't know about that," I say. "It might not be anything against you, but more that he can't let go."

She cups the amethyst. "Decent-sized stone. Thanks."

"You're welcome." I grab a couple more cookies for the ride home. Then I toss the backpack over my shoulder. It clunks heavily against my right hip.

We walk to the front door. "You're doing an awesome job with the robotics club. Everyone knows it, Claire. Even people from other schools."

She ducks her head, but not before I catch a glimpse of a small smile.

Outside, I climb onto my bike.

The countdown is on.

Nine hours till midnight.

chapter
thirty-five

I manage to stumble through the rest of the afternoon and actually read over the science study notes Junie and I wrote. Just in case Polly knows what she's talking about.

After dinner, I play video games with Sam, who bugs me for details about the ghost hunting.

"Überboring," I lie.

Josh calls when he gets home from practice. "So, Sherry, last night was way weird."

And tonight will be way weirder. But I'm not up for a supernatural discussion, which will lead to a massive panic attack on my part. So not good for detecting. "Yup, way weird," I say without adding any comments.

"Yeah, anyway, Nick is helping me with math on Friday," Josh says. "Then he and Junie want to do something with you and me that evening. My mom said we can chill at our house."

Listen to my boy, planning a fun double date. Except for the Nick part. Which I am getting over for Junie's sake.

After I flip my phone closed, there's a couple more minutes where I'm still floating with good boyfriend feelings. Slowly, though, they leak out, like when Coke goes flat. And I'm left nervous and jittery and worried about Sun Cemetery.

The Ruler goes to bed at her regular crazy third-grader hour. Sam hits the sack too. He says he's catching a cold. I didn't even notice him sneezing or coughing. I hope he's not turning into a hypochondriac.

I head upstairs. I'm killing time till Junie shows. And I may as well lounge with my fish.

I open my bedroom door. There's a faint whiff of honey + dirty socks. Dylan was in my room!

Ack! Eek! Ike!

And then I spot her. Poor little Cindy, flopping on the floor, her silvery tail twisting and turning, her cute little fishy mouth opening and closing.

My heart hammering, I race to her, scoop her up in both hands and plop her into the tank.

Prince zips right to her, nudging her with his

236

handsome head. She gives a little flip. The two of them smile up at me and swim off.

The aquarium lid is lying by my bed. I grab it up and snap it back on. I never ever remove the lid, because bala sharks love to leap out of water.

Dylan tried to murder Prince and Cindy!

I am so talking him into the silver box. He's done messing with The Ruler. He's done messing with my fish. He's done messing with my life.

It's about eleven, and Junie and I are kneeling on the sidewalk in front of my house. We're under the streetlight. It's gloomy and dim, but we're trying to save our flashlight batteries.

Our voices low, we're dividing the stuff I took from Claire's living room. The sidewalk looks diseased, with all these odd-shaped shadowy lumps.

"Any trouble sneaking out?" I ask.

"Not really. It helps that my parents go to bed after the ten o'clock news and always sleep with the ceiling fan on." Junie straightens her shoulders, enjoying her detective status. "Plus, I used the side door since their bedroom's at the back of the house."

"You're a natural." I give a nervous giggle. "Maybe we should open a private-eye business when we grow up."

"Yeah, right." She leans forward and picks up a couple of the lumps. She waves them at me. "Uh, Sherry?"

I squint into the darkness. The Popsicle-stick craft and the bronzed baby shoe. "I grabbed a little of everything."

"And you brought us snacks?"

I squint some more. She's holding the peanut butter and honey sandwiches I made.

"They're not for eating." I tell her about Dylan's pre-competition rituals with the sandwiches and the socks.

Junie pats the ground, feeling around. "I'll take the coffee beans." She pauses. "Because he'll, uh, I'll probably be, uh, more free to call your mom." She pauses again. "If we even have to."

My insides feel like I swallowed the entire Hoover Dam with water whooshing over it. "Junie, I'm scared. I don't think I can pull this off."

She stops cramming the cruise picture into her backpack. "Sherry, you're good at talking to people and figuring them out." She pushes the photo in the rest of the way, then zips up her pack. "I wish I could be more help. But I can't see him or hear him or anything."

"I know." I stand and hoist my backpack on. In some ways, even with Junie there, I'm basically on my own.

There's a whiff of coffee. "Hi, girls. Any time you're ready," my mother says.

Grandpa flaps in and perches on my shoulder. "Let's go."

Junie and I hop on our bikes and get pedaling.

By the strong smell of coffee, I can tell Mom's flying between us. "What's in your backpacks, girls?"

"A bit of this and a bit of that." I name the objects.

"Good job, Sherry," Mom says. "And you have flashlights?"

"We have flashlights," I say.

All leaning forward on her handlebars, Junie's huffing and puffing. She manages to nod.

"Extra batteries?" Mom asks. The questions are really only directed at me. The whole world's aware of Junie's super organizational powers. "The espresso coffee beans?"

"Chill, Mom. We're on it."

We're quiet, each lost in our own thoughts. A few cars drive by us. But mostly all you hear is our lungs sucking in air, our pedals creaking and our tires squelching on the pavement.

"The. Cemetery. Never. Seemed. This. Far. Away." Junie's face shines in the dark.

I bend down and rub my calf. "I'm getting some serious leg cramps."

Junie doesn't even answer. Unless you count heavy breathing.

"Earlier today, Grandpa and I found a small woods on the opposite side of the cemetery from the entrance," Mom says. "That's where we'll wait. We'll be far enough away that Dylan won't sense us, but close

239

enough that if you coffee-call, we can fly over in a flash."

I fill Junie in on where Mom and Grandpa plan to hang out. "Mom, what exactly can you do to him? I mean, he's got more power than you."

"Mrs. Howard is coming for backup," Mom says.

"But if she bails us out," I say, "we don't get credit for solving the mystery."

"Sherry, keeping you and Junie safe is more important than class credits. Even more important than Real Time." Her voice is heavy with emotion. "I want Real Time too, where we can sit and talk face to face, like . . . we used to. But I'm not willing to risk your life or Junie's." She swallows. "So if Dylan starts to lose control, I want you to promise you'll call me. Immediately."

All tight and tense, I nod.

"Mrs. Howard is the mistress of the silver box," Grandpa croaks.

I stop pedaling and coast to give Junie a chance to catch up. While she's gasping and catching her breath, I tell her about Mrs. Howard.

Junie slows to a stop and clambers off her bike, her feet thudding heavily on the road. "Who knew there were so many hills on the way?"

I climb off my bike too.

"And you've got the silver box?" Mom asks.

I pat my pocket. "Right here." I'm constantly aware of it pressing into my thigh.

Junie and I stop wheeling our bikes. There, in front of us, is a big Sun Cemetery sign and a drive with a chain across it. We're at the entrance.

"This is where Grandpa and I leave you two," Mom says. "Remember, if for *any* reason you feel you need us, call."

I repeat this to Junie.

She nods.

There's the faintest feathery squeeze on my shoulder. Mom! Grandpa waves a tattered wing.

And they're gone.

It's dark and creepy. We're a couple of teens armed with backpacks full of ordinary objects, a plastic bag of coffee beans and a magic silver box. Yikes.

We push our bikes over to the chain. Then we slide under, dragging the bikes after us.

The lights on our handlebars throw off dim, wobbly beams that stretch into long, quivering shadows. The palm trees rattle in the breeze. A cemetery at night is überspooky. And I so don't do spooky.

My hands sweaty, my pulse pounding, I force myself to keep moving forward. When all I want to do is race home.

Before we get to the gravestones, we reach a little garden area with a stone bench and a floodlight shining from a nearby pole. There's no moon, but we won't need our flashlights.

"I'm not going any farther." I lean my bike against the back of the bench.

"Sounds good to me." Junie drops her bike in the grass.

Cross-legged on the ground, we start hauling Greene family treasures from our backpacks. The air feels thick with danger. There's no honey + socks smell. Yet.

Junie and I chat nonstop about nothing. To fill in the silence. To keep an ongoing link between us. Anything to keep from getting totally creeped out.

I'm naming the objects as I pull them out. Like my backpack's a big party grab bag. "Oh, here's a shiny soccer trophy. And look at this little tiny baby shoe."

There are times in life when the sound of human voices is more important than the words. This is one of those times. Our silly conversation feels like a big, comfy blanket that's wrapping around us and keeping us safe.

On the stone bench, I start building a little stalker shrine. The tall stuff in the middle, with some small stuff to the right and some small stuff to the left. I place the sandwiches in front.

Junie follows my lead, listing everything she hands to me. She plays along, all singsongy. Like nothing's bizarro or out of the ordinary. Like we often spend a school night in the cemetery, piling somebody's junk

242

up on a bench. In the hopes their mean ghost will show up and agree to getting squished up in a metal box. And sent on his merry way to wherever.

Then Junie clams up.

And the silence separates us, like someone threw up a brick wall.

"Sherry?" Her voice is high and squeaky. "Do you have the coffee beans?"

I shove my hand back in my pack and feel around. Nada. "I thought you had them."

"I think I left them on the sidewalk in front of your house."

We both jump up, like the ground suddenly heated up to volcano temperatures.

We're in front of a shrine, constructed specifically to summon a nasty ghost-stalker. And we don't have any coffee beans to call for help. We're two standing ducks.

Junie hops on her bike. "We have to ride to your house and get them."

I grab my bike. "And be back here by midnight."

"We can make it if we don't walk up any of the hills," Junie says.

My leg is in the air, halfway through the arc that will carry it over my bike seat to the ground on the other side.

Unfortunately, I don't make it.

chapter
thirty-six

When you're unathletic, something as simple as climbing on a bike can trip you up.

Instead of my leg arcing over the bike seat, my foot jams against it. Hard. I tumble backward, twisting my body around to land on my front. I stick my hands out to break the fall.

Ouchie ouchie mama.

Best-case scenario: I have broken only one wrist.

Worst-case scenario: I have broken both wrists, both legs, both hips, and all my fingers and toes.

Junie drops her bike and sprints over to me. "Are you okay?"

I explain the two scenarios to her.

All doctorish, she orders me to stand and walk and wiggle my fingers and toes. Quickly. Because a ghost-stalker is on the way. Because the clock is ticking closer and closer to midnight.

When we get to the left wrist, I gasp and whimper.

"I bet it's broken," Junie says. "It's swelling and your hand's twisted kind of funny. At least it's your left; you can still take the science test."

With my right hand, I press on my left wrist, massaging it feather-gently. I yelp. "This is the worst pain of my entire life." My eyes swim in tears. "No way I can ride my bike. No way I can even ride on the back of yours. What're we going to do?"

"Can you smell Dylan yet?" Junie asks.

I stick my nose in the air and sniff. "No."

"Okay. You stay here. And sit." Junie claps for each point. "Move as little as possible. I'll get the beans."

"Don't leave me." My voice wavers. "We can handle Dylan together, without Mom and Grandpa."

She touches my shoulder. "Sherry, I'm next to useless. I can't hear him, or smell him, or see him." She's talking fast and breathless. "But the second I find the beans, I'll summon your mom. As soon as she spots me by myself, in front of your house, waving the bag of beans, she'll know you need help desperately. If your grandfather happens to arrive before her, I'll tell him. Then I'll speed back."

"Junie?"

She leans in close, her worried-best-friend face right next to mine.

"Pedal faster this time," I say.

Junie runs her bike to the chain, flings it under, then jumps on and soars down the drive. All that's missing is a superhero cape billowing out behind her.

I drag myself over to the bench, carefully cradling my wrist. Then I sit down, lean back, close my eyes and gulp baby breaths. The stiller I am, the less I feel like I'm at death's door.

"Sherry?"

Ack! Eek! Ike!

My eyelids jerk open. "Sam!"

From behind a nearby bush emerges a dark blur of a brother. Perched on his bicycle, his toes scrape along the bumpy ground, slowly propelling him forward. "Sherry, are you okay?" His forehead is crinkled with concern.

"What are you doing here?" I shriek.

"I heard you and Junie talking in the office today. So I came to help trap the bad-guy ghost."

"Are you out of your mind?" I shriek again. "Get out of here, Sam. Go catch up to Junie." I point with my good arm.

"Do you really think your wrist is broken?" His voice is small.

With the back of my hand, I rub sweat off my

forehead. Sweat from pain. Sweat from fear. "Yeah, I do. But you gotta leave, Sam."

He sets his lips in a thin determined line.

"Go! Home! Now!" In my agitation, I jostle my arm. I bite back a scream. Sam will never leave if he figures out how much agony I'm in.

"Where'd Junie go?" he asks.

"To get magic beans."

"Magic beans!" Sam says. And the fact that he swallows this bizarro paranormal explanation so easily only goes to prove how much he bought into Harry Potter. "Where are they?"

"Under the streetlight in front of our house," I say.

Suddenly, all goes still. The small breeze dies. Every blade of grass stands perfectly stiff at attention. Every leaf freezes. Maybe even the blood has ceased swimming in my veins.

From somewhere, a clock starts gonging midnight.

The silver box hums in my pocket.

The smell of honey + dirty socks swirls gently through the air.

"Get out of here!" I scream at Sam. "Go home!"

Sam crosses his stubborn twiggy arms over his stubborn sunken chest and plops down on his stubborn bony butt. "I'm not leaving my big sister with a broken wrist all alone in a cemetery to face an evil ghost."

Sam, my math-whiz younger brother, responds to

logic. Not to screaming. I switch tacks. "I need you for a very, very important task. It's not something I'd normally ask my *younger* brother to do. But with this wrist . . ."

His face goes all intent and focused, like a cat getting ready to spring.

"It's the beans. You've seen Junie ride a bike?"

He nods.

"You're, like, a thousand times faster. Even with the head start she's had, you could easily pass her and leave her in the dust."

He stands, arms straight at his sides. Like a soldier awaiting orders.

The sickly smell of honey + dirty socks is stronger.

It takes all my willpower to speak slowly and evenly. "When you get to the beans, open the bag and hold it up high above your head. The magic beans will banish the ghost."

He grabs his bike, hops on and is gone, a hair before the twelfth clock gong.

The ghost-stalker's smell surrounds me. The silver box is fighting to get out of my pocket. My wrist throbs like it's going to fall off. The last gong echoes.

It's midnight.

chapter
thirty-seven

"**S**o, this is how you got me here," Dylan says. "Impressive." The Popsicle-stick craft thingie floats in the air. "My pencil holder from Boy Scouts."

Boy Scouts? I was thinking preschool. Hard to believe he went from that lame pencil holder to award-winning robots.

"So, did you get Ms. Paulson to quit robotics?" He gales around me, chilly like air-conditioning. "Is that why you summoned me?"

I sit up straighter, getting ready for business. The small movement wrenches my wrist. I squeeze my eyes shut briefly, to get a handle on the pain.

I position my broken wrist on my stomach and

slowly walk my good hand into my pocket. The silver box is cold. I ease it out.

"*You* brought the silver box?" Dylan's voice hikes up in shock. "What kind of freak are you?"

"I'm a freak?" I'd put my hands on my hips, if I could. "This from a ghost who won't move on. Who just hangs around bugging people."

"You're not talking me in." Dylan spits out the words. The box is dull. Not one single sparkle glints off it.

"Why *won't* you move on?" I say. "Don't you have better things to do?"

"Better than making sure the Donner Dynamos beat Saguaro?" Dylan truly sounds shocked, like he never considered there might be more to life after death. "I want to see the Dynamos back on top and at the world championships for robotics." The team buttons flip over on the bench where he's examining them. "Which means we need your school's team to take a nosedive."

"So you thought poltergeisting The Ruler, er, Ms. Paulson would freak her out and she'd quit mentoring the Saguaro team?" I say. "In a million years that would never happen. She doesn't do backing down. She's kind of a terrier that way. I speak from experience."

"I have more plans for her."

I shiver at his words. And yelp at the wrist pain. A one-armed negotiation is not for sissies.

"Why'd you overfeed my fish and take the lid off

their tank?" My blood boils at the thought. "Fish! Innocent fish!"

"Because you were a mole on my team."

"I never did anything bad. I'm useless at robotics." I roll my eyes. "You know what, Dylan? You are a bully. You bullied Ms. Paulson and you bullied me and you bullied my fish."

"I have a cause." Dylan sounds defensive. "Winning at robotics is important for Donner."

"Winning by cheating isn't the same as plain old straight-out winning." The silver box is warm, like banana bread just out of the oven. "Besides, cheating is unfair to Claire." The box gleams.

"Really?" he says, a huge question mark in his voice. Like I've said something he never considered before.

"Claire saw your outline last night at Donner. Did you know that?"

"No," Dylan says, the *o* all drawn out. "She saw me?" He pauses. "For real?"

"For real." I pause, thinking Sam must be halfway to the beans, which means I need to talk Dylan into the silver box quickly, before my mom and grandpa show up. I hold the box a little higher in the air.

"What was she doing at school so late?" he says.

"Checking on the robot. She knew something was up with its performance at the practice competition."

"Wow." He's impressed.

"She's working hard, Dylan." The box is hot. One end cracks open. "She wants to be just like you and take the Donner Dynamos all the way to the world championships."

"She can't." I can just imagine him frowning and shaking his head.

"She can. If not this year, then next year. You don't give her enough credit. Probably because she's your little sister," I say. "Lots of people believe in her. She's smart. She's dedicated. She gets the importance of bling on a robot."

"Yeah, but there's knowledge and a whole philosophy I didn't get a chance to pass on to her," Dylan says.

A philosophy of robotics? Puhleeze. I think we're taking ourselves a little seriously here.

Dylan must still be at the shrine because the cruise photo, the picture with his entire family, hangs in the air.

The silver box sizzles. I try to visualize Sam's whereabouts. Three-fourths of the way to our house?

"I met your mom." I hug my wrist in closer.

"You saw my mom?" Dylan asks wistfully.

"She seems really nice. A great baker too. I love her frownies."

The silver box glows and sparkles and bounces up and down on my palm.

Dylan's waiting for me to make the next move. He must sense it'll be huge.

He's right.

It is huge.

I know exactly how to talk him into the silver box.

chapter
thirty-eight

Sometimes, even when you know what to do, you don't want to do it. Sometimes, you have something someone else needs more than you. But it still kills you to give it up. This is one of those times.

"You miss Claire?" I say.

"Uh-huh," Dylan says.

"And you have unfinished robotics business to share with her?"

"Uh-huh."

I take a deep, shaky breath. This is it. Once I say it, there's no going back.

The box glitters and shines, the brightest it's ever been. Like it was polished up for this very moment. This moment of connection for me, the box and Dylan.

"I'll give you my five minutes of Real Time," I say quietly.

No response.

"If you go in the silver box. Willingly. With the intention of moving on after."

Still no response.

"You know what Real Time is, right?"

Still no response.

There's a gentle breeze that moves above me. I look up to see Dylan's shape. His face is vague but visible. He's sad and emotional with glistening eyes. "Every ghost knows what Real Time is," he says softly, like dew on grass. "It's like the Holy Grail for us."

"The Holy Grail? My dad watches that movie. Monty Python. Or Ponty Mython. Or—"

"Why're you doing this for me, Sherry?"

I sigh. "You need it more than I do. To help you move on."

There's a whisper of a thank-you as a tornado of air whizzes around me. The air is thick with the smell of honey + dirty socks. Then, tail first, the tornado spirals toward the silver box. With a click, the lid flips wide open. A white light shines from within. The tornado leaps into the light. The light and the tornado spin down into the box. The lid snaps shut.

The silver box settles, completely still on my one good palm. Protecting its precious cargo.

Whoosh. Whoosh. Flap.

Smells of coffee and cinnamon rolls announce the arrival of my mom and Mrs. Howard. Grandpa lands on the grass beside me.

Mrs. Howard tweezers the box gently from my grasp.

I force myself to let go. The box is all proud and polished like silverware ready for Christmas dinner.

"Thank you, Sherry," Mrs. Howard says. "Congratulations, you did it."

"Pumpkin, you are amazing," Mom says.

"Good job," Grandpa croaks.

"How difficult did you find it?" Mrs. Howard asks.

I shake my head, my throat closing up. Finally, I cough out, "It cost me."

"It always does, honey," Mrs. Howard says sadly. "It always does."

Tears pool in my eyes. "He was mean to The Ruler and my fish. But now I know him and I get him. He had to let go of all that anger and give Claire a decent shot at robotics without his shadow hanging over her. Still . . ." Tears roll down my face, and my throat's totally closed so that I can't choke out any more words.

Mrs. Howard rubs my back. "You did a wonderful thing for him, honey. You freed him. He was lucky to have you. And I think you got something valuable from the experience too." She rises in the air. "I need to get Dylan to Dairy Queen." Looking over her plump shoulder, she says, "Don't worry about returning the

Greenes' belongings. I'll send someone from the Academy to take care of that."

Maybe she can send someone over on Saturdays to clean my room too.

As Mrs. Howard flies off, the silver box twinkles in the night sky like Tinkerbell winging her way to Never-Never Land.

Mom's right by me. "Tell me about Sam. Why was he holding up the coffee beans? How did he get involved?"

I explain how he was eavesdropping when Mom, Junie and me were in the office, discussing the mystery. And how he snuck out tonight to help in the cemetery, then rode fast to get the left-behind coffee beans.

"I'm so proud." Mom sniffs. "My kids are watching out for each other."

Then, Mom and Grandpa go on to say all the right ego-building things about how I'm this talented person who succeeded at this incredibly difficult task. I'm pretty sure Grandpa croaks, "Good work, Sherry," not "You're a jerk, Sherry." Which wouldn't make sense at all. Anyway, I just keeping nodding and saying thank you while I swell up to the bursting point with pride.

Because I'm sitting so still, soaking up the compliments, I forget about my wrist and go to stand. I scream.

"Sherry, what happened?" Mom says in the voice I associate with Band-Aids and Popsicles and cuddles on the couch.

"I tripped getting on my bike. My wrist really, really hurts. I'm sure it's broken and I'll have to go to the hospital." I swallow. "I better call Junie and find out where she and Sam are."

Then I'll call The Ruler.

And face the music.

chapter
thirty-nine

The Ruler, Sam and I don't get home from the hospital until way late. Turns out I do have a broken wrist. Our long and painful wait at the emergency room gave The Ruler tons of time to let me know how disappointed she is in my sneaky behavior. Little does she realize that the field trip to Sun Cemetery protected her from the evil plots of a ghost-stalker. Instead of blasting me from here to Canada, she should be slinging gift cards my way.

Then again, saving someone before they even know they're in danger might be the best kind of saving. I think maybe it is.

Quite frankly, I am limp with exhaustion. It is shocking to see how much I've aged. I have dark circles under my eyes like someone drew on me with thick black marker. And my skin has this green, sickly alien-ish hue. I look at least twenty. Maybe twenty-one.

Even The Ruler cannot argue with the fact that I'm a mess. Plus, I advise her once or twice of how much my wrist aches.

In the end, she decides that she and Sam will go to school in the morning. I'll stay home.

I trudge upstairs. My knees go weak with happiness at the sight of my room and my fish. I'm home. I did it. I'm only partially broken.

Tap. Tap. Tap.

Grandpa's at the window. "You're okay?" he croaks.

I hold up my waterproof pink cast. At least with my fashion creativity, it won't take much finagling to work this baby into my wardrobe. "Cool enough?"

He nods his raggedy head. "Your mom and I were worried. I said I'd fly over and check on you."

That is by far the absolute longest sentence from Grandpa I've ever understood. "Grandpa, can I give you a note for Mrs. Howard?"

He nods again.

I explain on my bubble-gum-scented notepaper how I gave my five minutes of Real Time to Dylan for use with Claire. In the hubbub of the cemetery, I'd totally forgotten to tell anyone about this.

Then I push aside the screen, enough to squeeze out the paper.

Before grasping my note, Grandpa says, "Grandma called me 'Wilhelm.'"

We high-five through the screen, a raggedy wing and my noninjured hand. "I'm so happy for you, Grandpa."

With my note poking out from his yellowed beak, Grandpa flaps off.

I hit the sack, where I sleep coma-hard. When I wake up, I have pillow lines denting my cheek and I'm all sweaty and starving and disoriented. I stumble into the shower, then down to the kitchen to grab up tons of food, especially items high in sugar.

I stick in my earbuds and click on my iPod till I'm listening to some ska that Josh uploaded for me. Then I'm sprawled on my bed, chatting to my fish. I bust open a sleeve of Girl Scout Thin Mints.

Dad phones. He skips his usual "How you doing, pumpkin?" to launch directly into a parental tirade on safety and trust and being the big sister. Bottom line: I'm grounded. Indefinitely. There will be an even more in-depth discussion next week when he gets home.

I bite my tongue and seethe. I wouldn't be surprised if steam is truly billowing out of my ears. Life is so unfair. Especially when you're part of a secret organization. I didn't want to go to the cemetery. I don't like dangerous and scary. I blink back hot tears.

"Has the world gone crazy?" Dad asks. "I leave on business for two weeks and get reports from home of slashed tires and broken wrists. What's next?"

After hanging up, I sit in a funk and stare at my pretty-in-pink arm.

Tap. Tap. Tap. Grandpa again. Probably bringing a thank-you note from Mrs. Howard. Surely *she* appreciates me.

I drag myself over to the window and slide it open. "Hi, Grandpa."

Perched on the outside ledge, he offers up a bunch of birdspeak.

It's frustrating how sometimes I can decipher his speech, but sometimes I can't. I guess this is an improvement on when I couldn't understand a word he said. "Mrs. Howard wants to see me?"

He nods.

I start muttering under my breath and stomping around my room. "I am so not solving another mystery right away. I have tests. I'm exhausted. I have a broken bone."

Grandpa taps on the glass again. "Now."

"Now?" And I'm back to muttering and stomping. "That woman is loco-crazy. Along with bossy and demanding." I look at Grandpa. "Wait. I'm grounded."

He frowns at me in a birdy way.

"Yeah, I know. Grounding doesn't apply to Academy business. Grounding is for normal kids with a normal existence," I grumble while trampling into the bathroom, where I throw on a black skirt, a polka-dot shirt and flip-flops.

This time I'm taking supplies. I one-handedly grab a box of aluminum foil and my bike helmet and jam them in my backpack. Then I hoof it to the bus stop. Honestly, I've gotten more exercise in the past week than I have in the past year of PE classes. I hope Josh likes muscular girls.

At Dairy Queen, I yank open the door and march to the back. Thankfully, I don't see anyone I know.

I strap on my bike helmet. And my oversized owlish sunglasses. I wrap my arms and legs with tinfoil. Not that this is easy with a broken wrist. But I'm determined. Once I'm outfitted, I push on the Employees Only door and step through.

Sparks fly everywhere, ricocheting off my tinfoiled arms and legs, shooting up to the ceiling, then showering down to the linoleum floor. No entry pain, thanks to a roll of aluminum foil.

Finally, they stop. I pull off my helmet and feel my hair. Fine. Not any wilder than usual. The bike helmet worked.

"Sherry, honey, you are so inventive," Mrs. Howard drawls. "Here at the Academy, we all surely love the way you think outside the box."

"Thanks," I say, pushing the sunglasses up to the top of my head. I wiggle out of my backpack and let it clatter to the floor.

"Are you exhausted after yesterday?" Mrs. Howard asks.

"Majorly. Which is why I'm not up for mysteries or investigating or anything else along those lines."

"Oh, honey, I didn't call you here to give you another case. No, no, no." With a long-nailed finger, she points at a Blizzard on the table. It slides obediently closer to me. "We are so impressed with your abilities, the way you talked Dylan Greene into the silver box. All the higher-ups are aware. And we'd just like to know that you'll make yourself available if that kind of situation arises again."

"But there's not a ghost to be talked in right now? You're not tricking me?"

"Absolutely not, dear. We just want to know you're available for the future."

"Well, probably," I say. I mean, this is pretty flattering. And I do love flattery.

"Wonderful, honey," she says. "One more thing. The Academy administration feels you should be rewarded for your unselfish behavior in offering up your Real Time to Dylan."

"Seriously?" I'm leaning forward.

"We're granting you five more minutes of Real Time."

I'm speechless. Which I don't think has ever happened before, outside the presence of Josh Morton.

"Is this satisfactory, honey?"

I'm nodding like a bobblehead.

I can't stop bobble-nodding. All that movement breaks loose a recent memory of my brother going mega stubborn and refusing to abandon me in the cemetery.

I open my mouth and out flies a suggestion.

chapter
forty

"I know Sam and I are grounded until Sam starts shaving," I say to The Ruler when they're home from school. "But if you think about it, that's a pretty unhealthy punishment." I put on a serious, logical face.

The Ruler looks up from the couch where she's typing on her laptop.

Sam stops reading and sets his book on the coffee table.

"What do you mean, Sherry?" The Ruler says.

"Being stuck in the same place day after day could stunt our emotional growth."

Obviously sensing this won't be a short conversation, she turns off her computer and folds down the screen. "Just last night, the two of you visited a cemetery. Sam attended school today, and you'll both be at school tomorrow. That's getting out and about."

I perch on the edge of the La-Z-Boy, keeping my back perfectly straight so she'll relate better to me. "I've been inside all day. I definitely need some exercise, which isn't easy given this." I jiggle my cast. "How about Sam and I walk to the bus stop, then ride over to Dairy Queen, where I'll buy him an ice cream out of my allowance. It'll stretch our legs, broaden our horizons and teach Sam about generosity. And"—I pause for dramatic effect—"I'll pick up some of that soy milk you love." End of rehearsed speech. Behind my ramrod back, I cross my fingers for luck.

Sam owl-blinks.

The Ruler's lips twitch at the corners. "Are you already feeling a little housebound, Sherry?"

"Maybe a little," I say.

"I do want to run over to school and see how this new code affects our robot's performance." Thinking, she places a finger on her bottom lip. "You'll take your cell phone? It will only be the two of you? You'll order small cones and not ruin your appetites for dinner?"

I nod after each of her questions.

Sam's still owl-blinking.

"Okay, then." The Ruler stands. "I'll drop you off at

Dairy Queen and pick you up after I've done a little robotic testing. I don't want you riding the bus so soon after breaking your wrist."

That is such a mom statement. Like climbing on a bus and a broken wrist are even related. I smile. "Thank you." With my good arm, I pull Sam to his feet and drag him, still stunned, through the front door.

The Ruler chitter-chatters about robotics for pretty much the entire drive. She really wants to figure out why the Saguaro bot let the Donner bot walk all over it at the practice competition. I wish I could tell her to let it go, that the Donner bot is now under control because Dylan's under control. But I can't.

She stops in front of Dairy Queen. "Is half an hour long enough?"

Actually, a little over five minutes is long enough. "Sure," I say, "or even less."

I'm pulling on the DQ door handle when Sam says, "What's going on, Sherry? I secretly follow you to a cemetery. We both end up grounded. But you're buying me ice cream? I don't get it." He plants himself between me and the door. "I'm not going in till you spill."

Ack. Eek. Ike.

Is it asking too much that I get this kid to his Real Time appointment?

I shrug, acting all nonchalant. "I just wanted out of the house, Sam. You're my excuse."

"Is Josh really meeting you here, and I'm your cover?"

Talk about your suspicious eight-year-old. No, no, no. This isn't even about me and my boyfriend. Just hustle yourself to the back room, little brother, and you'll get to hang with Mom. Sure, you won't remember it. But a part of your brain won't forget it either.

I paste on a fake scowl. "Josh might show. But keep it to yourself."

He smiles and scoots through the door. "Okay, but it'll cost you a large Chocolate Chip Cookie Dough Blizzard."

I think the same overly pregnant woman from last Friday is still standing in front of the Oreo Brownie Earthquake poster.

Once we have our treats, I herd Sam toward the rear of the restaurant, where we easily find a booth. Just like Mrs. Howard promised, it's empty.

I pick off a wedge of chocolate shell from my dipped cone.

With a grin, Sam dips his plastic spoon into his Blizzard.

My cone in my left hand, I use my right hand to fold a napkin into smaller and smaller squares.

With each fold, an incredibly cool feeling mushrooms inside me. I am giving Sam a gift. Which he doesn't even know about. And somehow that makes it even more amazing.

Cinnamon and sugar tickle my nose and Mrs. Howard hazily materializes beside me. "It's time, Sherry. You can wait at the front of the store."

"Hey, Sam, I'm gonna get some water." I stand.

He nods, all busy and noisy, scooping up his Blizzard.

I back away slowly, my eyes on his face. Mrs. Howard stays by me.

Sam's cheeks are puffy, full of his frozen treat, when the smell of coffee wafts into the back room. The bench seat across from him, where I was sitting, sinks a little. An invisible someone picks up the napkin I was fiddling with and continues folding it.

Sam startles and gazes up, like he heard his name. The spoon drops from his grasp. He beams. Hugely. You could turn off all the lights, and DQ would still be lit up.

"Hi, Mom!" Sam says. "Did you get off work early?"

And he has this look on his face that kids get when there's a surprise. Like if the ice cream truck unexpectedly drives up your street in the winter and your mom lets you buy a treat. Giddy and happy and excited. A look I haven't seen much on Sam's face since our mom died. A look I helped give him today.

"Sherry's here too," Sam says. "She actually bought this Blizzard for me."

I can't hear my mom's response.

Sam nods. "Yeah, she is a great sister."

Mrs. Howard prods me in the small of my back. "Let's give them some privacy."

I plod through Dairy Queen and out the door, then flop cross-legged on the sidewalk. I twirl strands of hair around my finger while my ice cream melts. Tears stream down my face.

chapter
forty-one

Saguaro Middle School is a hotbed of gossip, and I'm usually in the know.

I return to school the next day, Friday, and learn a couple of newsworthy items.

First off, Candy's now tutoring Kyle in English. And they're an item. This is not a case of opposites attract. This is a case of similar mean people attracting. The entire student body is happy because Kyle and Candy will keep each other busy and out of everyone else's business.

Second, Earring Girl, one of the cool eighth graders, stops me while I'm crossing the courtyard. "Sherry, right?"

"Yeah." I'm eyeing her absolutely adorable scoop-neck T-shirt. It's dotted with a gazillion rosebuds. "Love your shirt."

Earring Girl grins big, practically from hoop to hoop. "Thanks. It's from the Rack. I'm doing all my clothes shopping there from now on."

I keep a smile glued on my face, but, uh, yikes. If all those eighth-grade girls do all their shopping at my store, the clothes will be über-picked-over.

"So I found out The Ruler is your stepmother." Earring Girl pulls down on her shirt and smoothes out the wrinkles. "And I owe you for the clothing tip. Here's the deal. Kyle's planning to big-time TP your house tonight."

"Thank you." I skip away, my brain churning out a really fun idea. A fun idea called "Kyle Is Foiled by a Mother Ghost and a Ghost Wren While TPing My House."

I skip all the way over to the giant stone saguaro statue, where I'm meeting Josh. He's already there, his back against the cactus. He swoops me up in a big, strong hug. I just hang for a second, enjoying the scent of chlorine + laundry soap and the warmth of his T-shirt. Finally, we break apart.

"Sherry, what's the deal with you and Junie going ghost hunting alone in the middle of the night?"

"It was a mixture of too much candy, too little sleep and a couple of crazy girls."

"I thought you were done with ghost stuff," Josh says.

"Yeah, well, we are now. Especially because we're both grounded."

"Bummer. For how long?"

"I think I can talk my dad and The Ruler into a week."

"That's it?" Josh takes a Sharpie from his back shorts pocket. "A week?"

"Because I'm gonna ace today's science test. Seriously, there's nothing about genomes and mitochondria and cell nuclei that I don't know."

"Impressive." He waves the Sharpie in the air. "I'm ready to sign your cast."

I stick out my arm.

He reads Sam's message aloud. " 'Einstein rules. Ghosts rule. Karate rules.' "

Then he tilts his head to read what The Ruler wrote. " 'Sherry, you make the world a better place.' "

Josh's flipping off the cap, when someone taps my shoulder. I turn.

"Can I sign?" Nick asks.

Josh hands Nick the marker, and I offer him my arm. I don't even hesitate. Because if my best friend, Junie Carter, thinks Nick is okay, well then, I'm gonna think Nick is okay. Junie is finally jumping on the social train, and I'm chugging right along with her. Besides, Nick and Junie are my ticket to the romantic world of double dating. After my science test. When I'm not grounded anymore.

Nick signs in cursive.

To Sherry, my new friend. Here's some free advice. Next time, take the bus.

I smile. Weakly. While I'm willing to chill with Nick, I can see it's not going to be easy schmeasy.

Junie jogs up. "My turn, my turn." She snatches the marker and leans against Nick, thinking. Then she writes, *Sherry, I will always be your partner in crime. Junie xo.*

She looks me straight in the eyes. "You okay?"

She's referring to the text I sent her earlier. The text where I explained how I gave my Real Time to Dylan. And how I gave my bonus Real Time to Sam.

"I'm totally okay." And I mean it. "So, guys, any ideas for our first double date? When Junie and I are off restriction, that is."

"What should we do?" Junie's so excited, her freckles are popping out.

"Let's TP Kyle's house. With loads of toilet paper, plastic forks in the lawn, Saran Wrap around the cars. The whole nine yards," I say.

"I'm in," Josh says. "I bet my mom'll drive."

"I've never done anything like this before," Nick says. "Double-dated or TPed." He grabs Junie's hand. "It'll be fun."

"My parents shop at Costco," Junie says. "I'll bring the toilet paper."

The bell rings. Junie and Nick scurry off to class.

Sharpie in his hand, Josh looks at me. "I didn't get to sign."

I hold up my cast.

He writes:

Sherry Holmes Baldwin, you're the best!